RACE

THE

NIGHT

Disney • HYPERION   LOS ANGELES   NEW YORK

RACE

THE

NIGHT

BY KIRSTEN HUBBARD

FIRST EDITION, NOVEMBER 2016
10 9 8 7 6 5 4 3 2 1
FAC-020093-16267
PRINTED IN THE UNITED STATES OF AMERICA
THIS BOOK IS SET IN 11.5 PT. JANSON TEXT
DESIGNED BY PHIL CAMINITI

LIBRARY OF CONGRESS CATALOGING-IN-PUBLICATION DATA
NAMES: HUBBARD, KIRSTEN, AUTHOR.
TITLE: RACE THE NIGHT / KIRSTEN HUBBARD.
DESCRIPTION: FIRST EDITION. | LOS ANGELES : NEW YORK :
DISNEY-HYPERION, 2016.
SUMMARY: "EIDER MIGHT BE LIVING AT THE END OF THE WORLD, BUT THAT
WON'T STOP HER FROM SEARCHING FOR THE THINGS THAT COULD MAKE IT
ALL BEGIN AGAIN—ESPECIALLY AFTER TEACHER ANNOUNCES A MYSTERIOUS
NEW TYPE OF LESSONS THAT TURN HER LIFE UPSIDE DOWN"— PROVIDED BY
PUBLISHER.
IDENTIFIERS: LCCN 2016002394 | ISBN 9781484708347 (HARDBACK)
SUBJECTS: | CYAC: ADVENTURE AND ADVENTURERS—FICTION. | BISAC:
JUVENILE FICTION / ACTION | ADVENTURE / GENERAL. | JUVENILE
FICTION / SOCIAL ISSUES / ADOLESCENCE.
CLASSIFICATION: LCC PZ7.H8584 RAC 2016 | DDC [FIC]—DC23
LC RECORD AVAILABLE AT HTTPS://LCCN.LOC.GOV/2016002394

REINFORCED BINDING

VISIT WWW.DISNEYBOOKS.COM

FOR ALL MY
IMAGINARY SISTERS

THE SEA THAT WAS

EIDER HADN'T SEEN THE SEA SINCE THE WORLD ENDED.

Maybe she'd seen it Before, but she couldn't remember. All she knew was the wanting, longing, *needing* to see the huge, crashing waves from her fairytale book face-to-face. To behold something with no end in sight.

When Teacher agreed to take her, she could hardly believe it.

"I just don't want you to get your hopes up, Eider," Teacher said. "I've told you time and again, there's nothing left."

It was hazy out, a slight wind stirring the dust in the air. Eider bit her thumbnail as Teacher started the van, which Eider had only ridden in once before. It had big, knobby tires for driving over the bumpy ground. A metal grate separated the backseat from the front, where the two of them sat.

The ranch disappeared behind them as they carved a meandering path through the desert sameness. In the sunlight, the world Beyond didn't look as dangerous as Teacher claimed it was. But it did look empty, with the exception of a few ancient telephone poles and the occasional ruined shack.

What if there really was nothing left?

They'd driven maybe half an hour when Eider saw it: the sea. Shimmering through the windshield like a slice of mirror. Almost as unreal as an illustration. Eider's belly tightened in nervousness or excitement. Sometimes they felt very similar.

Teacher pulled up at the end of the road. Just a stretch of sand between them and the water, and after that, the horizon blurring into the sky. She kept the engine running, probably for the cold air.

"Go on," she said. "I'll wait right here."

"Really?" Eider asked.

"It's all right. I've seen it many times before."

Whether Teacher meant before or Before, Eider didn't know.

She noticed the smell as soon as she stepped out of the van. A sulphury punch that made her screw up her face.

The sand crunched under her feet. When she knelt and sifted her hands through it, she discovered it wasn't sand, but crushed fish bones. Skulls ground to pebbles. Teeny tiny ribs. Spines snapped to bits.

And as she drew closer to the sea, she realized it wasn't the clear blue of her fairytale book. It seemed sick, with great big splotches of green and brown. And waves? Barely any. The foam along the shoreline looked like spit, clogged with more dead fish. Some were newly dead, with round staring eyes and goopy fish flesh.

That explained the stink.

No mermaids lived there, that was for sure. Or dolphins or starfish or anything else. Unless Eider's feet were crunching their bones, too.

She hurried back to the van where Teacher waited.

"How was it?" Teacher asked.

Eider glanced at the sea one last time. "It's incredible!" she said. "Everything I hoped it would be and more."

Teacher smiled.

Eider knew she wasn't fooled one bit.

—

Eider stared out the window as they drove to the desert ranch, the van's knobby tires bumping over the desert sameness. Pleated earth and scraggly brush. Beige nothingness as far as she could see—and as far back as she could remember.

Teacher patted Eider's shoulder. "I'm sorry."

"It's okay," she replied, chewing her thumbnail.

"That's why it's better not to see," Teacher said, her

voice kind. "So the happy image you hold in your head won't be replaced. That way, you'll always picture things the way they were Before."

Eider nodded, even though she couldn't remember the sea Before. Only what it looked like in her fairytale book—but Teacher didn't know she still had that.

"You have so much potential, Eider. That's why this phase has been so disappointing. Now that the sea is out of your system, do you think you'll finally be ready to focus on your lessons?"

Eider knew there was only one possible answer. "Yes, I do."

She didn't say what she was really thinking: that a phase is only a phase if it ends at some point. If it doesn't—isn't it just who you are?

When they arrived back at the desert ranch, Eider expected the other kids to clamor around her, badgering her with questions. That's what she would have done. She even had answers ready—answers that made the sea sound better:

I've never seen anything so big!

There were fish everywhere!

Yeah, I'll never forget that seashore smell!

But nobody seemed particularly interested. Just like when she'd asked them to go with her in the first place. Then, Linnet had been too scared, as usual. Eider hadn't even bothered with Jay, but she'd poked Finch in his scrawny side, the way Avis did. "Maybe we'll find some amazing stuff!" Nope.

And in the storage room, she'd shown Avis the double-page spread in her fairytale book with the ocean and mermaids. "Look! It'll be so beautiful."

"I can't believe you still have that," Avis had said, flipping her rust-colored braid over her shoulder. "And no, it won't be beautiful. Don't you get it, Eider? There's nothing left."

"We don't know that for sure."

"Yes we do. Teacher's told us time and again."

"But there's got to be *something*. Something different than all of this." Eider had opened both arms grandly, as if taking in the desert sameness.

"All of what? The storage room?"

"You know what I'm talking about. There's got to be something besides the desert ranch. Something more."

"Yeah, right."

Eider had sighed. Avis was Eider's best friend, but sometimes that felt like one of the only things they had in common. It wasn't that Avis didn't wonder about the world Before, like Eider did. It wasn't that she didn't long for something different. But for Avis, all that longing was the same as daydreaming. A game of pretend.

"Seriously, is that the only reason you want to go?" Avis had asked. "Just in case Teacher's wrong?"

"No! Not *wrong*—mistaken. But . . ." Feeling

discouraged, Eider had shrugged. "I just think it'll be interesting, is all."

She hadn't been able to tell Avis the real reason:

Robin.

—

Robin had never seen the sea either. But she'd talked about it often.

Starfish and dolphins. Narwhals and puffins. Barracudas and great white sharks. And mermaids—always mermaids. Robin had loved mermaids the most.

The kids at the desert ranch weren't family, Teacher had told them. They were better than family. But Robin was the only kid who *looked* like Eider. She had Eider's black hair. Her large, dark eyes. Her dusky olive skin that turned even browner in the sun, while Avis's and Finch's skin reddened first. Linnet's was dark already. The resemblance made Eider feel special.

Nobody else had a sister.

In Eider's memories-that-weren't, she and Robin sat on the cement slabs and talked about mermaids. Which fish they ate. If all that salty seawater made them thirsty. How they went pee. "The same way fishes do!" Eider said.

Robin's laugh sounded exactly like Eider's.

Of course they knew mermaids were make-believe, like all the stories in their fairytale book. But sometimes, *everything* seemed like make-believe. Everything they read about in books and learned about in lessons. Automobiles and ballroom dancing. Circuses and pumpkin coaches. Animals with names like armadillo and opossum and pangolin. Music. Families.

Unlike mermaids, they were all things that had existed, once upon a time.

All things that used to be.

Sometimes, it was hard to believe. That once upon a time, there was a whole wide world outside the desert ranch, filled with things beyond Eider's wildest dreams and even beyonder than that. Hard to believe—but thrilling, too.

That there were towns and cities.

That there were soaring gold-colored bridges and buildings that scraped the sky. There was a sea with huge, crashing waves. There were cookies!

But not anymore.

"Maybe the sea never changed when the world ended. Maybe the mermaids are just waiting for everything to get fixed. And then they'll dive out of the sea—"

"Dive out of the sea?"

"They'll dive right out onto the rocks, where they'll sit and comb their hair."

"And maybe that'll be the start again."

"The start of everything good again."

"The beginning of the beginning."

Eider should have known better. Teacher had told the

kids time and again there was no world Beyond the desert ranch—or nothing worth visiting, anyway. The desert ranch was the only safe place left.

But it felt so good to believe that something else existed—no matter how dusty and hot it got, no matter how cold and endless the nights, no matter how distant the desert ranch seemed from the whole wide world Before.

Eider should have known better.

Since Robin had never existed, either.

2

THE DESERT RANCH

EIDER KEPT HOPING AVIS WOULD ASK ABOUT THE SEA, but she didn't. Not that evening. Not the next morning at breakfast (stale cornflakes and powdered milk, yuck), or as they walked to the classroom for Practical.

"What's up with this wind?" Avis asked instead.

Eider shrugged. "I don't know."

"Well, it's driving me bananas."

Behind them, Linnet giggled. At ten, she was two years younger than the other kids and paralyzingly timid. Even when Eider openly invited her to chat or play, she hung back.

"It's worse than yesterday, don't you think?" Avis went on. "My poor hair."

Eider glanced at her best friend. Avis's hair was coppery brown, the color of old pennies. Her braid was longer than Eider's dark one—though Nurse cut them at the same

…ne, Avis's grew much faster. Which was perfect, because Avis loved brushing and braiding her hair. She loved anything pretty, really. That was why Eider had hoped calling the sea beautiful would interest her.

"Yeah," Eider said. "The air was really hazy at the—"

"I hope it lets up before Physical," Avis interrupted. "Or else we're gonna be panting dust."

Linnet giggled again.

Eider sighed.

—

Even though the world had ended, Teacher said structure was important. Even more important than Before.

Not everything at the desert ranch had structure. There could be fun, too—like during Free Play. Or when Teacher or Nurse shared a funny memory at Circle Time.

But in the past three years, structure had kept increasing, until Eider began to notice the bones of it everywhere. In the fence that circled the ranch and its padlocked gate. In the boots and overalls the kids wore, even on the hottest days. During their twice-monthly checkups with Nurse. Most of all, in their lessons: Physical and Practical.

Practical lessons took place in the classroom. Teacher sat at the head of the table, so everybody could see her and she could see everybody. That was how she liked it.

"Did everyone sleep well last night?" she asked.

Everyone nodded. Including Eider, though she hadn't slept well at all. She rarely did, but last night, sea dreams kept sloshing her awake.

"Good," Teacher said. "Without quality sleep, you'll never reach your full potential. Eight hours per night is ideal. Does anyone know why?"

Teacher was tall, with long white hair bound in a braid as thick and coarse as rope. The sun had cooked her skin into leathery folds, like tortoise hide. She'd seen a lot of daylight, and darkness, too. When she looked at you, it was hard to look away.

Even if you really, really wanted to.

Eider didn't know much about Teacher's life Before. The memories Teacher had shared at Circle Time felt distant, like old-timey illustrations. She knew a lot, though. She could answer any question—probably even the ones she didn't seem to want to.

If anyone had a chance of catching up to Teacher, it was Finch, who was already raising his hand. He remembered everything he'd ever read. Including all the books they used to have.

"Circadian rhythms," Finch said confidently.

"That's right," Teacher said. "Can you explain to the other kids what circadian rhythms are?"

"They're the clocks inside your body," he replied. "The systems that tell you when you're supposed to be asleep and awake."

"Unless you don't get enough sleep at night," Teacher added. "Then you're likely to nod off during lessons. Right, Eider?"

Eider sat up straighter.

"Very good, Finch." Teacher smiled at him.

Finch nodded, but he didn't smile back. That was nothing unusual. His resting face was a frown. But anytime he grinned, it spread from his face onto everyone else's like a happiness disease.

A smile wasn't the kind of thing you could charm from Finch, though. It had to come from the inside. Usually when he'd figured out something. Not just anything— something difficult. Something that had kept him hunched over his notebook an entire afternoon, until suddenly he'd sit up and exclaim, "Oh!" Then came his grin. Big, wide, goofy-toothed. And instantly, everyone around him would start grinning too, even Teacher.

"Circadian rhythms aren't the only secret abilities your bodies have," Teacher went on. "Some you use daily or nightly. Others more rarely. Still others, you probably haven't even discovered yet."

"Like what?" Avis asked.

Teacher waved her hand, dismissing the question, as she often did. It was Eider's least favorite gesture. "Tonight, I want you to make sure you get quality sleep. Our next lesson will take place at night."

"While we're sleeping?" Jay asked in his dopey tree-trunk voice. His questions were always the stupidest.

"Raise your hand, Jay. And no, of course not. You'll stay up late for this lesson."

Eider felt her spirits lift a bit. A night lesson was something different, at least.

"Now, onto the World Book." Teacher pulled out a hardcover volume and placed it on the center of the table. This one's spine said Q–R, but all the R pages were secured with a binder clip.

Finch raised his hand. "How much longer until we get to the letter *R*?"

"Not many words begin with *Q*. So not much longer."

"How long, exactly?"

"Finch," Teacher said. There was an edge to her voice now.

"Sorry," he mumbled.

Teacher opened the World Book. "Let's begin. Avis, I bet you'll enjoy this section: *Queens*. How about you read first?"

"Sure!" Avis beamed.

The World Books had maroon-and-black covers, with pages edged in gold. Nearly every letter of the alphabet had its own thick, hardcover volume. The books looked very ancient. Almost magical, even though they didn't have any magic inside them, unlike the books the kids used to have. No stories, only facts. And a lot of the facts were boring—a thought Eider kept to herself, of course.

Eider kept lots of things to herself.

Like how she wondered about the missing pages.

Sometimes, the World Books jumped straight from page 242, for example, to page 247. Whenever they came to one of the gaps, Eider couldn't help wondering what they'd never get to learn.

———

As the kids trudged up the rise after lunch, the wind picked up. It strummed the earth in hushed, haunted tones, tickling their hair with ghostly fingers.

Eider had a complicated relationship with the wind. Windy days could be awful—the kids didn't just pant dust, but ate it and drank it, too. Windy evenings, when the sky thickened into a deep gray haze, were just as bad. Eider hated not being able to see out. It made her feel like the desert ranch really *was* the only thing left.

But Eider couldn't truly hate the wind. The windier it was, the more likely she'd find a secret paper.

Papers didn't come with every wind, or even with most of them. The desert ranch was a planet in a universe of empty space, after all. But every once in a while, when the winds blew just right, a paper raced across that endless emptiness all the way to the desert ranch.

And every once in a while, Eider found it.

"Hey, Eider," Finch said, startling her from her thoughts.

"Hey, Finch. What's up?"

He ran a hand through his hair. It was so pale, it

looked like the color had been frightened out of it. "I was wonder—" he began.

Before Finch could finish, Jay crashed into both of them. "Looks like we've got another obstacle course," he bellowed. "Get prepared to lick my dirt, losers."

"Watch it," Finch said.

"Or else what? You gonna bore me to death with your circular rhythmics?"

"They're called circadian—" Finch sighed. "Never mind."

Jay hooted loudly.

Eider rolled her eyes. She'd decided maybe if she ignored Jay enough, he'd go away. It hadn't happened yet, but she was optimistic.

There were two types of Physical lessons: Structured and Free Play. Free Play was everyone's favorite. The kids could take part in any activity they wanted, as long as they kept moving: kickball, tag, pretend games.

During Structured, Teacher chose their activities and observed them. The cooler the day, the more intense the workout. Like navigating the obstacle course. Or jogging around the inside of the fence until Eider's sides felt pinched by invisible hands. When summer peaked, they'd hide in the classroom with the swamp coolers blowing and do stretches, or roll a ball around.

But today wasn't too hot, and Jay had been right about the obstacle course. All five kids stood at the start of it, arms crossed.

"Finch, you're up first," Teacher said. She held a clip-board and a stopwatch, as usual. "Ready. Set. Go."

Finch might have been the smartest kid at the desert ranch. But his strength was all in his head, not in his gawky, too-tall body. Even his first step was clumsy: he almost missed the tire.

Eider looked away. The rise they were standing on wasn't that high, but she could still see the entire ranch from up here. Their entire lives.

She saw the old concrete buildings where they ate and learned, and the trailers where they slept. The twin wind-mills, which provided most of the ranch's electricity. The solar panels on the rooftops, which gave them the rest.

The grove of date palms, which offered much-needed shade and chewy, bland fruits. The well where they got their water. Teacher's office. Beside it stood the metal spike, yet another artifact left over from Before. The spike was the tallest thing at the desert ranch. It had its own fence around it, and a rusty old sign:

NO TRESPASSING
KEEP OUT

And then there was the main fence, stretching all the way around the desert ranch. Some of it was barbed wire. Some of it was chain-link. In other places, it was scraps of wood nailed together.

Teacher used to say the fence was symbolic—that it only existed to separate the desert ranch from the nothing Beyond. But over the last three years, the Handyman had made the fence much stronger and taller.

If you wanted to find a place to cross to the other side, you really had to look.

Avis slung an arm around Eider's shoulder. "I'm awfully tired of these obstacle courses," she said. "Is it just me, or are they getting easier?"

Eider shrugged, glancing at Teacher to make sure she hadn't heard Avis's comment. Then again, it might impress her, like most things Avis did.

"Avis!" Teacher called. "Ready? Go."

Out of all the kids at the desert ranch, Avis was the most agile. Eider watched her pound through the tires, *hop hop hop*. Grab the rope and hoist herself up. Swing from bar to bar to bar. Avis always made Teacher proud.

"Very good, Avis!" Teacher marked her clipboard. "Jay! Ready? Go."

Jay took off. With his big, meaty hands and brawny shoulders, he was the strongest by far. He never let anybody forget it.

"What's the holdup, slowpoke?" he'd shout at Linnet. "C'mon, monkey arms!" he'd bark at Finch. "Wasted all your breath on talking, huh?" he'd holler at Avis. "Wake up, cloudface!" he'd yell at Eider.

"Jay," Teacher often warned.

But as far as Eider knew, Teacher had never disciplined him. Maybe because she didn't realize he could be outright cruel—something Eider knew from the collection of animal skeletons he kept under his bed. Any meanness Teacher saw could also be interpreted as confidence.

And confidence meant the kids were trying. They were realizing their potential. They cared—unlike Eider.

Eider *wanted* to do well. She *wanted* Teacher to be proud of her, so badly. But ever since she'd woken from her rattlesnake fever and found out Robin had been imaginary, everything felt like too much trouble.

Lessons. Checkups. Even Circle Time.

Robin had never been real. But still, losing her felt like an amputation. Like missing a leg or an arm.

No, it felt like half of Eider's heart was missing. And her entire being suffered for it. Her emotions. Her strength. Her energy. She didn't have enough blood pumping through her body, that was why. She'd never catch up, with fifty percent of a heart.

"Very good, Jay," Teacher said. "Eider!"

Eider took a deep breath.

"Ready? Go."

She ran.

3

FAIRYTALES

LIFE WAS GOOD AT THE DESERT RANCH. Teacher reminded them, time and again.

"You're the luckiest kids in the world," she said. "You're brilliant and special and purehearted. Most of all, you're important. Without you, there'd be no hope for the world. Because you are the whole world now."

Sometimes that did make Eider feel important. Like the entire scroll of world history had unfurled all for them.

Other times she felt differently. Because if they were the only people left, why did it matter if they were important? What was the point?

Eider wanted there to be a point.

Really, really badly.

But a point didn't have to be a big thing, like the sea. Or a sister. It could be something as small as a book.

Specifically, a fairytale book kept under a floorboard in the storage room.

—

During Quiet Time the next evening, Eider wiggled the loose floorboard until it opened like a creaky door. Her penlight's glow revealed Cinderella in her pumpkin coach, glass slippers sparkling.

"Hey there," Eider greeted her.

She flipped through the stories of goblin rats and mermaids and pumpkin coaches, straight past the final page of the final story. Then came a bunch of blank pages—pages now filled with Eider's wind-gifted papers.

Her secret papers weren't make-believe, like the fairytale stories, but real. Real like the facts in the World Book. Realer than the World Book, actually, because they weren't just explanations of the world before. They were *from* Before.

She didn't find them often. Every month or so, although one thrilling week she'd found three. Most were very small. Just scraps, really, smaller than the papers they used in the outhouses. Some listed odd-looking words in faded ink with numbers beside them:

```
CABBAGE BNCH . . . $0.99
SWS HOT CHOCLTE . . . $3.49
TIL CHEDDAR 2LB . . . $6.89
```

Eider's favorite paper was a stiff rectangle. A postcard, she recalled from the Mail section in World Book M. The front was a glossy image of a beach. The sea was bright blue—just like in Eider's mermaid story!—and the sand nearly white. Right in the center sat a bright pink drink in a stemmed glass that resembled a desert flower.

The back had handwriting on it:

Dear Roland,
Bet you could use one of these right now! Wish you were here.
Love,
Mandy

Roland and Mandy. Eider had thought about them lots of times. Mandy and Roland. Dear Roland, Love Mandy. She wondered if Roland had been waiting for the glossy rectangle, and if Mandy had assumed he'd received it. If, somewhere between the sending and receiving, the world had ended.

She wondered how many letters the end of the world had interrupted.

Once, after a windstorm that had lasted two whole days, Eider had found a long, skinny paper with a round hole in the top. It wanted her to eat a bunch of odd-looking bundles called "sushi," a word Eider had no idea how to pronounce.

Suh-shee? Soosh-ee? Suss-high?

Unlike the unfamiliar terms in the World Book, Eider

couldn't ask Teacher about sushi. She didn't want Teacher to know about the papers she collected. Or that she still had the fairytale book. Teacher would take the book away, like she had all the others, and Eider would never see her papers ever again.

In the dark, she traced their words with her penlight. Whispering them out loud, like magic spells sent from Before.

Rap. Rap. Rap.

Eider almost dropped her book. Nobody had ever knocked on the storage room door. Even in the daytime, it wasn't the sort of place where a person knocked before entering—they usually strode right in, seeking a jar of pickles or a shovel.

"Hold on!"

She slid the book back under the floorboard. When she opened the door, she found Finch outside, shuffling his feet. The sunset gave his hair a pinkish glow.

"Hey, Eider," he said. "I thought I saw you head over here. What are you up to?"

"That's none of your business," she said.

Finch frowned. "Oh. . . . Sorry. I can go."

Eider felt bad. She'd never felt particularly close to Finch, but he wasn't the sort to tell on her for sneaking. "No, it's okay. I just come here to think sometimes."

"About the sea?"

She blinked in surprise. "Well, a little bit. Yeah."

"You really saw it?"

"Yeah . . . I really did." She joined him outside, closing the door behind her.

"What was it like?"

It was the question Eider had been dying for somebody to ask. And Finch, of all people, was asking it. Straitlaced, unimaginative Finch, who wouldn't know a mermaid from a rotten fish. Who spent Free Play tinkering with metal scraps. Or studying his notebooks—and *enjoying* it.

She remembered all the answers she'd prepared about the sea:

I've never seen anything so big!

There were fish everywhere!

Yeah, I'll never forget that seashore smell!

But she found herself telling Finch the truth instead. "It was . . . Really, it was nothing. I mean, it was huge! Don't get me wrong. But it had all gone bad."

"The water?"

"Yeah. It was brown and mucky. And stinky, too. And the fish—"

"There were fish?"

"Dead fish. They were all dead, as far as I could tell."

"So Teacher was right."

Eider nodded.

She and Finch glanced at each other, then away. There seemed to be a lot of things they weren't saying. Like how they'd both wondered if Teacher had been mistaken about something. Even though she hadn't been.

But Eider also felt a little encouraged. Turned out she

wasn't the only kid at the desert ranch who wondered about Beyond.

She opened her mouth to speak. "I—"

Eeeeeee. Eeeeeee. Eeeeeee.

The alarm.

It was a high-pitched whine, like a mosquito scream amplified. A sound the kids knew well—and hated. It meant danger. Or, more frequently, the *potential* of danger.

"Let's go," Finch said.

Eider glanced at the storage room, hoping she'd replaced the floorboard securely. Then she ran for the shelter.

———

Teacher called the shelter their safe place. "No matter what kind of danger arrives," she'd told the kids, "you'll be safe inside the shelter."

From the outside, it didn't look like much. Just a rooftop the color of desert sameness, and a slanted doorway with steps leading down. But as soon as the kids shut the door, the darkness made it distinct. Even in the daytime. The only openings to the outside world were narrow windows obscured by thick, black screens.

Usually, the alarm was just a drill. A couple times, there'd been an actual danger—but it had passed. Drill or danger, the kids never knew until afterward, when Nurse released them. And he never told them what the danger was.

"All that matters is that we're safe!" he'd say.

Drills were very serious, Teacher told them time and again.

But they were also boring. Sometimes, they went on so long the kids fell asleep. This time, Jay didn't even wait. He sprawled facedown on a cushion and, moments later, started snoring.

"Such an oaf." Avis scowled at him, then sat on a cushion beside Eider. "What do the rest of you want to do?"

"I wish we had our notebooks," Finch said. "Then we could get *Q* over with."

"What have you got against *Q*?" Avis asked, poking him in the side with her penlight.

Finch swatted at her hand. "Nothing. There are just a lot of words that begin with *R*. I think it'll be more interesting."

Eider could only think of one word that began with *R*, and it was the only word she wasn't supposed to say. The scar on her ankle twinged. She reached down and scratched it, searching her brain for other *R* words.

"I think all the letters are interesting," Linnet said quietly.

"You would," Avis said.

The younger girl flushed.

"We've got even better letters coming up soon, though," Avis continued. "Weird ones, like *W*. And *X* and *Z*."

"*Z* is the final letter," Finch said.

"Raven!" Eider said triumphantly.

Finch glanced at her. "Huh?"

"Never mind. What do you guys think we'll do after we finish studying *Z*?"

"I guess we'll know everything then," Avis said. "Or maybe we'll start at *A* again. It's been a couple years—all I remember is, like . . . airplanes."

Airplanes flew over the desert ranch from time to time, but there was nobody inside them. They flew automatically. Another *A* word.

"Agriculture," Eider said.

"What do you remember about agriculture?" Avis asked.

Eider shrugged.

"Everything," Finch said.

Avis poked him again. "Nobody asked you, Finchy. We already know your brain's made of prickers and glue."

"Art," Linnet said.

Eider smiled at her. "I'll bet you remember lots about that."

When the kids were younger, Teacher used to give them paper and markers for drawing. They'd all enjoyed it, but Linnet had loved it the most, filling page after page with cactus blooms and coyote faces and funny doodles of the other kids.

Now, all they had were their notebooks, and those were just for Practical. "We should be more conservative about paper," Teacher had announced. "And only use it for important things." Art didn't seem to count.

The kids continued to chatter animatedly, then more

slowly. Linnet was the second to fall asleep, curled into a ball like a storybook kitten. Avis was third. Eider didn't feel sleepy yet. She leaned her head against the wall, wondering what was going on outside.

"What was it you were going to say?" Finch whispered.

Eider glanced at him. "When?"

"Before the alarm sounded."

She thought back. "Oh. Just that . . ." It seemed strange to say it now, locked inside this cramped space. "I still think there could be something out there. You know? Something left. I'm always waiting for—I'm always keeping my eyes open."

They both glanced at the shelter door.

"You're just waiting for something to come to you?" Finch asked.

"No, not exactly . . ."

The sound of a key in the lock shut Eider up. She nudged Avis and Linnet, while Finch woke Jay. "Go away," Jay muttered. Then his eyes widened.

Teacher stood in the doorway, holding a lantern.

Eider's eyes widened, too. Nurse always came to get them, not Teacher. Had the danger been real?

"Just a drill," Teacher said. "Sorry it ran on so long."

All the kids let out their breath. But Teacher didn't hold open the door, the way Nurse did. Instead, she stepped inside the shelter and switched off her lantern.

"It's time for our night lesson," she said.

4 THE NIGHT LESSON

"DOES EVERYBODY HAVE THEIR LIGHTS?" Teacher asked.

The kids all nodded. Their penlights lit their faces from below, making them look slightly ghoulish.

"Good." Teacher closed the shelter door behind her. "Now turn them off."

Five clicks and then darkness. Total darkness. Eider couldn't see Avis beside her, or Teacher before her, or even her own hand in front of her face. She could have been anywhere at all. That was a strange thought.

"Darkness is an interesting thing," Teacher said. "Technically, it's just the absence of light. Right, Finch?"

"Right," Finch replied, his disembodied voice somewhere to Eider's right.

"It feels like more than that, though, doesn't it? Almost like it has a presence. A power of its own."

Eider nodded, even though nobody could see her.

"Even during new moons, or on overcast nights, the darkness isn't complete. Not like it is in here."

Eider opened her eyes, then shut them, then opened them again. No difference.

The darkness was complete.

"But it only affects our eyes," Teacher went on. "And fortunately for us, the human body is a complex thing. It compensates. When one sense shuts off, the other senses kick in even stronger—if you let them, that is."

"Let them?" Avis repeated, then paused. "I raised my hand."

"You must go deep within yourself. Give power to your senses. Everybody listen for a minute. Hold your breath if you must."

Eider held her breath and listened.

At first, all she heard was silence. That same heavy, desert silence she knew so well.

But with nothing but darkness to distract her, Eider began to notice other sounds, too. The clatter of wind-tickled pebbles. The screech of crickets. The sound of a door closing, far off—it must have been Nurse, leaving his office.

"What do you smell?" Teacher asked.

Nothing, really. Eider breathed in and thought. Breathed out and thought. The harder she concentrated, the more she noticed the different flavors in the air. The salty sharpness of sagebrush and creosote. The other kids' breath. The musty dusty forever scent of the desert all around them.

"There's a whole lot going on," Teacher said, "isn't there? More than you ever realized. The sounds were always there—it's just easier to find them in the dark."

"The darkness helps?" Avis asked.

"It helps us focus. Life is full of distractions—even here, in the middle of the desert. Sounds and sights and smells, all competing for attention. Sensory overload!"

Linnet giggled, then covered her mouth.

"But we have much more control than we think. It's all about choosing what signals we tune in to. Like turning a radio knob. White noise sharpening into the essentials we need to hear, to see, to know."

Eider liked that. It made her feel more powerful, some-how. Even if the power was only over herself.

"Now, what do you see?"

"Nothing," Jay said. "The lights are off."

"Jay," Teacher warned.

But Jay was right. Eider couldn't see anything. How could any of them? It was pitch-black inside the shelter, without even a speck of light. . . .

"Look harder," Teacher said. "Be patient. I have faith in you kids."

Patiently, Eider looked harder.

And then . . . she realized she *could* see. Not much. But

she could make out the shadowy ghosts of her fingers when she wiggled them in front of her face. A moment later, she could see Avis doing the same thing beside her.

"See anything now?" Teacher asked.

Everybody said they could. Well, everybody except Jay, who was still grumbling that he couldn't see.

"Be patient," Linnet whispered.

Jay quit grumbling. After a few seconds, Eider heard him say, "Oh."

"So the darkness isn't complete, after all," Teacher said. "Maybe it never was. The power to overcome it was always inside you. Because you're brilliant and special. You're different. You are *more*."

A thrill stirred in Eider's chest.

"And you've just had your first Extrasensory lesson," Teacher said.

"Extrasensory?" Finch said. "What's that?"

"A new kind of lesson. I've been planning it for a long, long time. But before I introduced it, I wanted to make sure you were ready. Until I knew every last one of you was focused on your lessons. Ready to look inward—instead of Beyond."

In the not-quite-complete darkness, Eider couldn't see Teacher's face. But she felt her gaze, just the same. Had Teacher been waiting on Eider this whole time?

Eider chewed her thumbnail, feeling ashamed. And a little guilty, too. Because despite what she'd told Teacher after their trip to the sea, she definitely wasn't finished looking Beyond.

"And you've all done very well," Teacher said. "Just like I knew you would."

With a click, Teacher's lantern illuminated everybody's face. The other kids were beaming, even Finch. Eider smiled a little, too. She couldn't help it.

"I'll explain more next time. But now, it's time for your reward."

Avis grabbed Eider's hand and squeezed. Rewards were rare but memorable. Like Eider's ballet slippers had been, before she'd lost them. She held her breath as Teacher opened the door and led the kids into the desert night, the desert sameness.

"Look up," Teacher said.

Eider looked up. And gasped.

The stars had come to life.

Sure, Eider had seen shooting stars before, when she remembered to watch the sky. But tonight, it was like the entire heavens were dancing. Pinging, zipping, rocketing, soaring. Eider's eyes danced too. She didn't even know where to look. It was like the parties she'd read about in the old books—a party in the sky, bright hot and white and golden blue, endlessly dancing, *dazzling*. So many stars.

We were the stars.

Eider inhaled sharply. She glanced around, but everyone else's face was still tilted upward.

The brightest stars in the whole sky.

A wave of dizziness hit her. She stared at the sky until her eyes watered, but that only made the dizzy feeling worse. So many stars. Too many stars.

Brighter than the sun.

Her knees began to shake, and she grabbed Avis to keep from collapsing. Avis thought she wanted to link arms. "So beautiful!" Avis said.

"It's like star soup," Linnet whispered behind them.

Eider squeezed her eyes shut. She was shaking now, not getting enough air.

"Hey, are you okay?" she heard Finch ask.

"Teacher!" Avis called. "Something's wrong with Eider. . . ."

Eider tried to hold on to the excitement of Extrasensory, the warmth of Teacher's pride, the dazzle of the stars.

But as the stars went black, all she could think about was Robin.

———

"The sky's a lot like the sea, don't you think?"

In Eider's memories-that-weren't, nighttime was all about stars. She and Robin would climb aboard the slabs, lie on their backs, and gaze up. Sneaking out at night hadn't felt like such a big deal then.

"I don't know. The sea is made of water and filled with living things. The sky is nothing but empty space."

"*It's not empty. Look all those stars!*"

"*Sure, but the space between them is still empty.*"

"*Doesn't matter. The stars are what's important. The space between them doesn't matter as long as they exist.*"

Eider couldn't always tell whose voice was whose. But it was Robin who put words to their biggest ideas. Robin who claimed they came from the stars.

"*We danced around up there. Jumped from star to star to star. We were stars. The brightest stars in the whole sky. Brighter than the sun.*"

Lying on the cement slabs with her sister, floating through the vastness of space, Eider believed.

"*Everyone had to squint when they looked at us. Or else they'd burn up.*"

They stayed at the slabs for hours. Almost falling asleep, but never quite. Enjoying the shared dream of stars and sisterhood.

But Eider had really been alone at the slabs, no matter how real her make-believe seemed. Just Eider and the imaginary waves and imaginary mermaids.

And her imaginary sister.

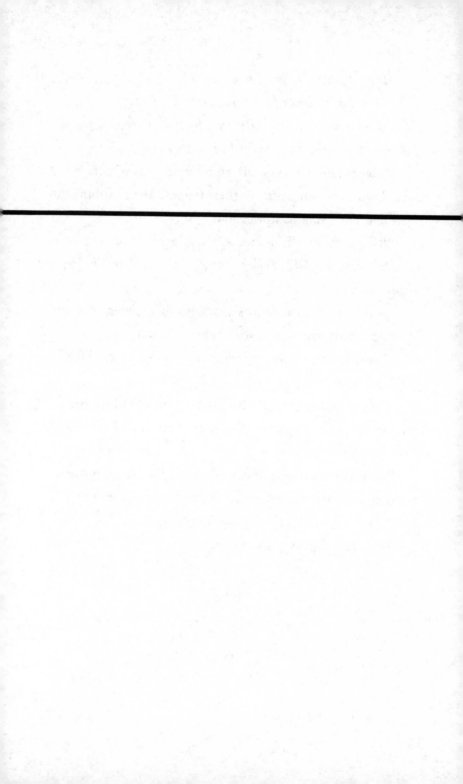

NONSENSE THINGS

EIDER WOKE TO DAYLIGHT, FEELING FOGGY. For a moment, she had no idea where she was.

"Hello?" she said, sitting up.

Then she noticed Nurse, dozing in a chair. Eider was lying on a cot in his office. Though the kids had check-ups every couple weeks, she hadn't been sick enough for bed rest in years. Not since she'd slept through ten days of fever—in this very same cot.

Eider's skin prickled. "Hey!" she shouted.

"What? Huh?" Nurse said, then noticed Eider. "Oopsie! Must have conked off."

Nurse was short and squat, with a bald, rather flat head. Once, Jay had said a giant had probably stepped on him as a baby. Eider had laughed, even though she liked Nurse. He was definitely loopy, but he was nice.

"You gave us a fright, there, kiddo," he said. "Feeling better?"

"What happened?" Eider asked.

"Teacher brought you here last night. It seems you had a bit of a spell."

"A spell?" She rubbed her eyes, but the fog remained.

"Teacher was very worried. So of course, I was worried too."

"I don't have a fever again, do I?"

"The thermometer said nope. But let's check again."

Eider watched Nurse unlock a cupboard. Each had its own tiny padlock—another form of structure, she supposed. Like the padlocks on the gate and on the door to Teacher's office. And the lock on the shelter door. . . .

Last night's events flashed through her fog in quick succession. The shelter, the night lesson, the Extrasensory announcement, the storm of falling stars. The memories-that-weren't, and after that, the dark.

"Did I say anything?" Eider asked worriedly. "Last night, when I had my spell?"

"Oh, only nonsense things," Nurse said.

"But . . . but did I talk about—"

"Under your tongue." He handed Eider a skinny glass tube.

With a little sigh, she did as he ordered.

Ever since her fever, Eider hadn't been able to talk about Robin to anyone. Not because she didn't want to—but because nobody would let her. They'd change the subject, the way Nurse just did. Avis would scoff or stamp her foot and say, "Eider, come *on*!" Finch would flush with silent discomfort. Linnet would burst into messy tears. Jay, though, had been the worst—he'd make fun of her or threaten to tell Teacher.

At first, Robin's name had slipped out often. Then less and less. When Eider finally buried her sister's name deep down, the entire desert seemed relieved.

But thoughts, of course, were harder to control. If Teacher knew how much Eider thought about Robin, she'd know Eider still wasn't fully focused on her lessons. That her phase wasn't over. Not even close.

"Let's have a look," Nurse said, removing the thermometer. He checked it, then smiled. "No fever. How are you feeling?"

"All better," Eider lied.

"Teacher will be so glad. And you won't have to miss lunch. I'm heating up your favorite: canned spaghetti."

Eider tried not to make a face. "Super."

"Enough for two helpings." Nurse winked. "It'll help you reach that famously elusive potential of yours."

———

Canned spaghetti wasn't the worst meal Nurse cooked, but it definitely wasn't Eider's favorite. Squishy noodles. Bright red sauce. She had to finish her entire bowl, just in case Teacher came around to check.

Teacher rarely ate in the dining area anymore, though. She almost always had important things to do in her office: "Work, work, work," she'd say.

Her absence meant Jay and Avis dominated every mealtime conversation. It was hard to say who was more obnoxious, although Eider would never have admitted that to Avis.

"Listen up, everyone!" Avis yelled, banging her fork on her mug. "We're playing a game. If we all changed into animals, what kinds would we be?"

"With that hair and face, you'd be an orangutang," Jay said, snickering.

"No, I wouldn't." Avis glared at him. "And it's orang-u*tan*, jerk."

"That's what I said. Orangutang."

"I know. And it's wrong. Right, Finch?"

Finch shrugged his narrow shoulders. He didn't like arguments. Neither did Linnet, who slouched in her seat.

Neither did Eider. In a world where all she wanted was a *point*, their same old bickering seemed so pointless. Then again, that was probably how Eider's fairytales seemed to Avis. And how her secret papers would seem, too.

Eider poked at her lunch. She thought of her sushi paper, its colorful little bundles. They didn't look edible, but at least they were cute, unlike the food at the desert ranch.

They ate what they got.

That's what Teacher told the kids, time and again, when they came across something tasty-looking in the World Book. Or when she shared a memory during Circle Time. "Fresh cookies," she'd said once, a faraway look in her eyes. "With chocolate chips that melted on your fingers. Now those were *delicious*. . . ."

"Maybe we can track some down," Nurse had suggested. "For the kiddos."

"Don't be ridiculous," Teacher had said. "There aren't any cookies left. We're lucky to eat what we get."

The storage rooms were packed with food, which never seemed to diminish. But all of it was old food, left over from Before. Which meant very little was *delicious*. Rice and spotted beans mixed together. Weird little sausages. Pancakes with no syrup. Pickles. Yellow soup with chicken squares and teeny tiny stars.

Star soup was pretty great, actually.

It probably wasn't *delicious*, but it was fun. Eider loved swirling it with a spoon until the stars surfaced, winking in and out of the yellow broth. Like last night's storm of stars. Or the falling stars she'd seen while lying on the slabs, gazing up . . .

"What about you, Eider?" Avis asked.

Eider looked over guiltily. "Huh?"

"*Huh?*" Jay mocked, then laughed.

"Ugh, you're so annoying." Avis threw a noodle at Jay, then turned to Eider. "If you were an animal, what would you be? Like, Finch would be a—"

"A rabbit!" Linnet exclaimed, giggling.

"Yep, a rabbit," Avis said. "Linnet would be a baby mouse. Jay would be a buffalo, obviously."

"What? That's not what I said!" Jay protested. "I said a wolverine!"

"Obviously a buffalo. So what would you be?"

"Maybe you could choose for me?"

"Okay." Avis pointed at Eider with her spaghetti fork. "You'd be a—"

"A penguin!" Jay interrupted. "A dreamy, stupid penguin, running off into the ice and snow."

Linnet covered her mouth.

"She would not," Avis argued. "Penguins can't fly. And if any of us could fly, it'd be Eider." She smiled at Eider. "I think you'd be a butterfly."

Eider wasn't sure about that, but she smiled back.

A BONE-DEEP KIND
OF WONDER

AS THE KIDS HEADED TO THE CLASSROOM AFTER LUNCH, an angry bark stabbed the air:

Woofwoofwoofwoofwoof

The Handyman had arrived.

Besides Teacher and Nurse, the Handyman was the only person they knew. Or saw, anyway, since he rarely spoke. He only came on occasion, to fix or deliver things. He lived outside the desert ranch, braving the dangers Beyond—which made him seem dangerous, too.

Oh, and he had a dog.

"Hi, dummy," Avis said.

The dog was tied up in the shade outside Teacher's office. It had black fur and yellow teeth. Its breath smelled like hot garbage. When it was excited, it would jump in a circle, over and over again, barking and barking and barking:

Woofwoofwoofwoofwoof

"Don't get so close," Eider said to Avis, who was making faces at it.

"Why? It's not going to do anything. It's too dumb."

Eider agreed that the dog was dumb, but a bite from it would still hurt. Even bites from smaller animals hurt. The scar on her ankle proved it. It looked like two pink, shiny eyes. Snake eyes, peering from inside her skin. "Shh. The Handyman might hear you."

They glanced at the Handyman's truck. He was reaching inside for something, his ropy arms even more sunbaked than Teacher's. Before he could look their way, Avis pulled Eider toward the classroom, giggling.

"Good afternoon, girls," Teacher said. She tugged on Avis's braid, then Eider's. "Feeling better today, Eider?"

Eider searched Teacher's face for disapproval and was relieved not to find it. "Definitely. Ready to focus on today's lesson."

"Glad to hear it. However, today's lesson won't start for a couple hours. I have some preparations to do first."

"Is it an Extrasensory lesson?" Avis asked.

"You got it." Teacher smiled. "Until then, you'll be having Free Play. I recommend a quiet indoor activity, so you won't be late."

Free Play! Eider really did intend to focus on her lessons—but suddenly, she was preoccupied by the familiar thrill in her toes, spreading upward. She used to be able to dance away the feeling, but now there was only one solution.

"What do you want to do?" Avis asked, as they walked away.

Teacher had only *recommended* an indoor activity, right? And a couple hours was definitely enough time. Eider could focus afterward.

"Because I've got a great new idea for a hairstyle," Avis continued.

"Actually, I thought I'd—"

"You know that old painting we saw in the Queens section? The one with the braids wrapped around her head? I want to try it on you." Avis raised an eyebrow. "You can read me your mermaid story if you want."

Eider hesitated, but only for a second. "Actually, I think I'm going to go—"

"On a walk," Avis finished for her. "In this heat? You're crazy!"

"It's not so bad."

"Plus, Teacher recommended an indoor activity. Sitting in front of the swamp cooler and doing hair sounds perfect. Except now I'll have to ask Linnet. And she yelps."

"That's not *her* fault." Avis wasn't very careful about pulling and pinching.

Avis smiled, then turned serious. "I hate that you go out there," she said. "Promise you'll be careful?"

"Always," Eider said.

—

Eider walked under the twin windmills and up the rise. At the top, she paused to look around. On hot, clear days like today, she could see more that *wasn't* the desert ranch than *was*.

But on windy, hazy days, it wasn't hard to believe the desert ranch was all that remained. A planet in a galaxy of empty space. An alien world of broken doors and abandoned rooms, of things that used to be but weren't anymore. Leaving the desert ranch was like stepping off the earth into the night sky.

Not something anybody in her right mind would ever do.

But Eider wasn't in her right mind. Probably because she hadn't just read her fairytale stories—she'd ingested them. Chewed them up and swallowed them. Now they lived in her body forever, a bone-deep kind of wonder.

And the only solution was to wander.

Finding the gap in the fence had been difficult. In fact, Eider had almost gotten caught. She'd been walking along the fence, pulling, pushing, searching for weak places. There weren't many—the Handyman had made it strong. And then:

"You're not planning on trying to leave us again?"

Eider had whirled around to find Teacher, standing just a few feet away. How long had she been watching? "No!" Eider exclaimed. "No, of course not."

"Then what are you up to?"

"Just . . . taking a walk."

"You weren't doing very much walking."

The tone of Teacher's voice had made Eider's heart pound. "I was also . . . looking," she'd said. "It's interesting to see what's outside the desert ranch. Even if—even if there isn't much out there."

"There isn't *anything* out there, Eider. There's nothing. And nobody."

Eider's rattlesnake scar had twinged. "I know," she'd said softly.

Then Teacher's expression had softened. She'd taken Eider's hand in her cool, callused one. "I just want to make sure you're looking inward instead of outward. You have so much potential, Eider."

After that, Eider had been a whole lot more careful. She didn't want to upset Teacher. Or worse, get disciplined.

Nobody knew exactly what discipline entailed. One time, the kids had sat around, speculating. Most of their guesses had been funny: a week of pickles for meals, copying the entire World Book by hand, kissing the mean dog on its stinky, slobbery lips. Jay's guesses, however, hadn't been funny at all. Being buried neck-deep in a red-ant pile. Spending a month locked in the shelter. Getting tied atop the spike like a human flag—at that, Linnet had started to cry, spoiling the game. But Jay's meanness had uncovered an important truth: as long as they didn't know what discipline was, it could be *anything*.

Eider tried her best not to think about it.

She paused at the date grove, the way she always did. Slipping into the trees for just a moment, then—when the coast was clear—sprinting for the fence. She located the gap where the nails had rusted and the old wood had splintered apart. Ducked her head. Took one step, then another . . .

And she was Beyond.

As always, Eider kept near the fence as she poked things with sticks, or nudged them with the toe of her boot. She turned over rocks and pushed aside scratchy plants. Peered into grooves of stone. Sometimes she even climbed into the ravines—just as long as she could still see the spike, rising high above Teacher's office. The only sound to break the heavy silence was the *crunch-crunch* of her boots.

Most of the junk Eider found, she tossed right back. But occasionally, she found something to keep. A roll of tape for securing her secret papers. Empty bottles with faded labels. Fabric scraps to bring Avis for her hair experiments.

Eider also found stuff for Finch's tinkering, though she could rarely guess what he'd find useful. He'd loved the tiny copper tube, for example, and the snarl of silver wires. He'd frowned at the tiny green toy soldier and the orange sock.

"What would I ever do with *that*?" Finch had asked.

"I have no idea," Eider had replied. "What did you do with the broken pair of scissors?"

Occasionally she found stuff she couldn't bring back. Like the huge, rectangular heap of coiled springs. Or the chair with a desk attached. The chair was orange and pebbly. The desk was small, with deep grooves gouged into its surface.

Eider had sat in the chair, pretending she was a student in a school from Before. Right away, she'd felt claustrophobic, the chair painfully stiff against her back. In her frenzy to escape, her legs had gotten stuck and the desk had toppled over. She'd had to crawl out on all fours.

When she thought back, it was kind of funny. She must have looked so silly. But nobody had been there to see.

Sometimes Eider wondered if there used to be a town here. Or a city. A huge city with skyscrapers and neon lights that blink-blink-blinked and fountains that spat rainbows into penny-filled pools, like the picture she'd seen in World Book F.

But Teacher said otherwise.

"People lived here, sure," she'd told Eider. "Long ago, before the world ended. But the closest town was far, the closest city even farther."

"How far?"

"Many, many miles west. Nearly eighty."

"Oh," Eider had said. "That *is* far."

Teacher had nodded. "But that's a good thing, Eider. Our remoteness is the very reason we're here. The reason we're safe. If we'd been in a city when the world had ended— well, we wouldn't be here. We wouldn't be anywhere. Just like the cities themselves, we wouldn't exist."

That notion had kept Eider from quality sleep for days.

It was getting late. Still, she walked and walked, zigging and zagging, never straying far from the fence. She didn't find anything interesting. Probably because she'd covered this ground a dozen times. How far had they gone when they'd run away? When they'd thought Other People might still be out there?

Not *they*, Eider reminded herself. She'd been Beyond too long—it was time to go. Shielding her eyes from the sun, she faced west one last time.

And saw a paper.

1

EXTRASENSORY

EIDER TOOK A FEW STEPS TOWARD THE PAPER. Then she stopped, her stomach sinking. It was only a bird. Flapping low across the desert, glossy-winged, nearly silent.

But wait—birds weren't that glossy. Or rectangular, for that matter.

A glossy rectangle? Definitely a paper! "Wait!" Eider called.

Whatever it was, it was getting away. Should she go after it? Had two hours passed? Maybe. Probably. If she was late for Extrasensory, Teacher would be disappointed. And if she realized Eider had been out Beyond the fence again . . .

She glanced toward the desert ranch.

Then she looked back at the paper, now a tiny dot in the desert sameness.

She threw out all caution and chased it. The paper dipped and whirled in the wind. It let her catch up, nearly grab it, then swirled away again, as if taunting her.

Finally, the paper got stuck in a patch of sagebrush. Eider grabbed it and stuffed it inside her overalls. As she sprinted toward the gap in the fence, she could feel the paper fluttering against her chest. Alive with possibility.

——

Eider found the rest of the kids gathered behind the classroom. No sign of Teacher yet, to her immense relief. She skidded to a stop beside Avis, trying to control her panting.

"What took you so long?" Avis demanded. "You're all sweaty."

Eider wiped her face with her arm, which was just as sweaty. "I know. I—"

"You went out too far. What if there'd been an alarm? And a real danger?"

"Shh," Eider said, even though the other kids were out of earshot. Avis was only a few months older than Eider, but sometimes she acted like her big sister. "I got here in time, didn't I? I always make it back."

"One time you didn't," Avis said.

It was the closest she'd come to bringing up—well, not Robin, because Robin only existed inside Eider's head. But the time Eider had run away. And everything that had come after. Eider's defensive feeling faded. She knew Avis was just being protective. "That's not going to happen again."

"Promise?" Avis asked.

Eider hesitated, then nodded without speaking. If she said it out loud, it would be real. She tried to save that for things she was one hundred percent certain about.

Teacher came around the corner then, already smiling. "This lesson's going to be a fun one," she said, opening a cloth bag. "Is everybody ready?"

The kids all nodded eagerly.

Teacher's eyes lingered an extra moment on Eider, still patting down her messy braid, before she continued. "Good. Our second Extrasensory lesson is about"—she pulled out a stack of cardboard squares—"mazes."

Mazes? Eider glanced at Avis, who looked confused. Jay raised his hand. "What have mazes got to do with seeing in the dark?"

"Nothing," Teacher replied. "And everything."

She passed out the cardboard squares. Each held a different, intricate maze, drawn with permanent marker. Using chalk, Teacher explained, the kids would have three chances to master the mazes while she clocked times with a stopwatch.

Jay and Linnet did all right. Better than Avis, anyway: "Those dead ends come out of nowhere," she muttered. Or, "I swear that wall wasn't there before." Eider thought she was doing pretty well herself. Then Teacher pulled out a blindfold.

"Now let's see how well you do."

Most of the results made the kids laugh. Avis's line was basically a scribble. Jay's, not much better. Linnet's slow, careful line made it two-thirds of the way through her maze, then fell off the cardboard. Teacher seemed less amused.

When it was Eider's turn, she concentrated hard. Pictured the maze behind her blinded eyes. She knew she was good at imagining, but even she was startled by her results—she'd only crossed the maze's walls a handful of times.

Finch went last. To nobody's surprise, he did best of all.

"Very good, Finch!" Teacher said. "You just might be a natural."

Finch grinned, so everyone else did, too. Even Avis, who'd been battling hard to maintain a scowl. "He was totally peeking," she muttered.

"Avis," Teacher warned. "Now, does anybody know what our first two Extrasensory lessons had in common?"

Jay raised his hand. "Not seeing?"

"Well, yes, but I want you to think deeper than that. The answer's in the word."

Finch raised his hand. "Extra senses!" he exclaimed. "Of course. Using senses other than the ones we ordinarily would."

"Exactly right." Teacher tousled his pale hair. "Extrasensory is all about discovering new abilities—but abilities you already have inside you. During each lesson, we'll test a different ability. Like we did with navigation and memorization today. That way, we'll determine which ones you're a natural at."

"What's a natural?" Avis asked.

"When you have a natural ability for something, and it doesn't take much training to master it. Think of it like learning languages—but languages you speak in your bones."

Suddenly, Eider felt very aware of her bones. She crossed her arms.

"You're the most brilliant and special children ever to have lived, after all." Teacher tucked the mazes back into her cloth bag. "And I'll bet you're hungry after all that concentrating. You're dismissed."

—

As she lay in bed, Eider wondered if she'd ever been a natural at something. The way Linnet was with art, or Finch was with building stuff. She couldn't think of anything. What about Before, when there'd been more options? Maybe Eider would have been a tuba prodigy—but tubas didn't exist anymore, so she'd never know.

She wondered if Finch could build her a tuba.

Unfortunately, she wasn't a natural at anything that counted now. Not Physical or Practical, that was for sure. Was that another reason she found it hard to care about them?

What activities *did* she care about?

She'd cared about dancing, before she'd lost her slippers. Reading stories in her fairytale book, and in the old books, when they'd had them. Exploring outside the fence. Finding things . . .

Like secret papers.

Eider sat up in bed. She felt around in her cubby for today's overalls. The rectangular paper was still in the pocket. Somehow, she'd forgotten about it.

She switched on her penlight and pushed back her covers.

"What's going on?" Avis murmured.

Eider switched off her light. "Oops. Sorry."

Unless she mastered seeing in the dark before morning, she'd have to wait until later. But for now, the promise was thrilling enough. With the paper under her pillow, Eider counted stars behind her eyes until she fell asleep.

FINCH WAS UNREASONABLY EXCITED ABOUT THE LETTER *R*.

"Let me guess why," Avis said, skipping in front of him on their way to the classroom. "Radishes? Royalty? Rabbits! You really do look like one."

"I do not," Finch said, trying to sound gruff. But his eagerness was still apparent in his bunny-like twitching.

"Rattlesnakes?" Linnet suggested, then instantly turned purple. "Sorry, Eider! I didn't mean to bring up rattle—" She slapped a hand over her mouth. "I'm so sorry."

"It's okay." Eider forced a smile. She was already feeling antsy, with her secret paper in her pocket. She'd had no alone time to read it yet.

"*S* is going to be real good," Jay said. "Spiders! Scorpions! And snakes—all the snakes, not just the ones with rattles. . . ."

"Knock it off, you creep," Avis said. "Everyone knows about your weird collection."

Jay scowled at her.

Teacher wasn't in the classroom when they arrived. But two things were waiting. First, five pieces of cardboard were pinned to the wall. Each had one of their names written on it in Teacher's spiky, all-caps handwriting.

Second, the World Book Q–R waited in the middle of the table. The *R* pages were free from the binder clip. Before anyone else could touch the book, Jay grabbed it and pulled it close to him. "Come and get it!" he hollered at Finch.

"Like you know how to read," Avis said.

"Jay, come on." Eider tried to tug the book from Jay, who wouldn't budge. "Please?"

"Please?" Linnet echoed in her tiny voice.

Jay exhaled loudly, then surrendered the book to Eider. She handed it to Finch, who accepted it with enthusiastic hands.

He flipped the first few pages. Then a few pages back. A couple forward. Then one back. One forward. His frown deepened. "Oh."

"Oh?" Eider repeated.

"The page is missing. The one I wanted."

"*Oh.*" It was a familiar letdown: flipping through the World Book and discovering a gap. "That's too bad. What were you looking for?"

"Nothing important."

Eider didn't believe him. But then Teacher entered the classroom, and there wasn't time for any more questions.

Instead of taking her seat at the head of the table, she stood by the cardboard names on the wall. "Before we get started," she said, "I wanted to make sure you've seen the results of yesterday's Extrasensory lesson."

The results? Eider glanced at the names again, now paying attention to their order:

FINCH
LINNET
EIDER
JAY
AVIS

"As you know, I've always documented your progress in lessons. But from now on, I'll be sharing it with you. That way, you'll see how you compare to everyone else. How much you need to improve at each skill we practice."

So Eider was third best at mazes? That didn't seem fair—she thought she'd done better than Linnet, anyway. She glanced at Finch, expecting a grin, but he only looked confused. Jay was seething. Avis slouched so low in her seat, all Eider saw was red hair and squinty eyes.

"Sit up, Avis," Teacher said. "I'm sure you'll do better next time."

Eider didn't know whether it was the rankings, or Extrasensory itself. But by Quiet Time that evening, she was still feeling irritable. She hoped the paper in her pocket would improve her mood.

As she hurried past the classroom, she saw Linnet sitting alone on the Circle Time rug, her penlight between her teeth. It was aimed at her notebook, where she was scribbling enthusiastically.

Curious, Eider crept up behind her. On the illuminated pages, she saw lines and squiggles. Something four-footed—a jackrabbit, maybe, or a fox. Whatever it was, it definitely wasn't World Book notes.

"Are you drawing?" she asked.

Linnet whirled around, wide-eyed. Her penlight fell into her lap. "No!" she said. "I'm only . . ." Her half-sentence hung in the air.

Eider smiled reassuringly. "It's okay."

"I'm not really supposed to."

"Because of the paper?"

Linnet shrugged. "I only use the backs of my notes, but . . . I still don't think Teacher would approve."

Eider didn't get it. Drawing seemed like the silliest thing in the world to disapprove of. But maybe Teacher disapproved *because* it was silly? A waste of time, like the stories in the old books? "Well, I'm not going to tell," Eider said.

"It doesn't matter. I'm tired anyway." Linnet scooped

up her penlight and notebook, hopped to her feet, and hurried away.

Eider watched her go, then continued toward the date grove. The palm trees rose from the desert sameness like a bouquet of flowers, almost as tall as the spike. During hot days, they provided welcome shade. There wasn't much of that at the desert ranch, other than the shadows cast by buildings and the occasional scrubby mesquite. But at night, the date palms made the darkness darker, and that was exactly what Eider needed.

Carefully, she stepped into the grove. She headed for the thickest part, where the fat, toothy trunks hunched closer together. The palm leaves drooped low, forming a sort of room where Eider could switch on her penlight and escape notice. She'd checked multiple times, leaving her penlight on and walking out, looking for the glow.

She sat with her back against a tree. Took a deep breath. Then she aimed her penlight at the glossy rectangle.

It was more than one paper; it was several sleek pages stapled together into a little book. A pamphlet, she thought it was called.

The first page read

Welcome Home!

in happy, swirly letters. Below the happy headline, there was an image of a family standing in the doorway of a big, peach-colored house. The family was waving. They had yellow hair, light skin, and the whitest teeth Eider had ever seen.

Her heart beat faster.

People. She was looking at pictures of Other People. Not illustrations, but actual people who had existed Before.

Eider flipped the page and found an image of another family: a different one, sitting on a sky-blue couch. A mother, a father, and two daughters. They had black hair and brown skin, like Eider's. That was their only resemblance to her, but for some reason, it gave her the chills.

She continued to read.

Your brand-new house awaits at Forest Gardens Housing Development! We work with banks to finance any budget! Come home to Forest Gardens, where your family's dreams will come true!

Eider turned the next page. *"Features,"* she read. Below, there was a list with tiny dots next to each line:

- *Central A/C!*
- *Huge front lawns!*
- *Community pool!*
- *Backyard gazebos!*

Eider didn't know what a gazebo was. Or even how to pronounce it, for that matter. *Gaze-bo? Gazz-ibo? Ga-zee-bo?* Or some other way?

- Stainless steel appliances!
- Wireless Internet!
- New laminate floors!

More unfamiliar terms. The map on the back didn't mean anything, either: just roads with numbers on them, a bridge, and a star that was circled by the letters *N*, *S*, *E*, and *W*. Feeling frustrated, Eider flipped the page and stared at the family again—the one with black hair, like hers. They smiled back at her. Unlike the yellow-haired family, their teeth were a perfectly normal color.

Deep inside Eider's chest, she felt a stirring. Not a memory-that-wasn't, but something even farther back. Gone before she could grasp it.

"Welcome home," she whispered.

———

For the second night in a row, Eider couldn't sleep. She tossed and turned, spun awake by her thoughts. About the wind-gifted pamphlet, and its glossy promises. About the families inside.

Teacher didn't control what the kids thought about. "It's impossible," she'd told them, time and again. "Nobody can control what you think. But I'm here to guide you. To help you look inward instead of outward. To help you focus your thoughts, instead of wasting them."

According to Teacher, many topics weren't even worth

thinking about. Some were frivolous or silly—like fairy-tales, for example. Some were very serious, like diseases and murder and war.

"You're too young to understand," she'd told them.

Other topics Teacher discouraged weren't silly or serious—just distasteful. Like family.

Family was *literally* distasteful, it seemed. When Teacher spoke about it, she acted like she'd eaten something unpleasant. A wormy date, or canned goods gone bad. Her mouth would twist, and her nose would wrinkle slightly.

"Did everyone have a family?" Avis had asked once during Circle Time. "Did we?"

"That's not the right question," Teacher had replied, waving her hand. "Because it doesn't matter. Families aren't anything special. They're common—or they were common, Before. People were born into them, without any choice. Or even if they got to choose . . . they chose wrong."

She'd paused a moment before continuing.

"But here, at the desert ranch? We're better than family. I'm more than a parent, or even a teacher—I'm your guardian. Your guide. That is much, much stronger. Just like the bond all of you share."

"Why is our bond stronger?" Eider had asked.

"Now *that's* the right question." Teacher had opened her arms like Mother Goose wings. "Because you were chosen—not only by me, but by fate. You were chosen to soar through the end of the world, and to land safely here at the desert ranch. You're the best, the most brilliant, the smartest, the most purehearted. And the luckiest.

"Who needs family when we are *so much more*?"

It made sense when Teacher spoke that way. That the kids at the desert ranch were better than family. That family wasn't even worth thinking about, since it didn't exist anymore.

But now that she'd seen the pamphlet, she couldn't stop.

She thought about fathers and mothers. Fathers and fathers. Uncles and great-grandmothers. Stepmothers. Stepdads. Cousins. Sisters. Families used to come in all shapes and sizes, she knew. Some families hadn't looked alike—but most families had. Like the families in the pamphlet.

Like Robin and Eider.

Robin and Eider, sitting together on a sky-blue couch, smiling. Part of a family.

Eider knew better, of course. But sometimes imagining felt just as good as believing.

THE FIRST STEP

THE NEXT DAY WAS COOLER. Clouds floated overhead like lazy birds, sometimes blocking the sun entirely. It was Eider's favorite kind of weather.

But when Teacher announced Free Play, Eider didn't know what to do.

She was feeling sad, that was the problem. Sad, and a little lonely. Probably the pamphlet's fault. From the rise, she watched Jay and Avis kick a ball back and forth, arguing the whole time.

"Is that the best you can do?" Jay taunted.

Avis stuck out her tongue. "Maybe if you watched your hooves, buffalo brain."

"Maybe if you watched your orangutang arms."

"It's orangutan! Gosh, you're hopeless."

They were annoying, as usual, but Eider still smiled a

bit. The sun came out from behind a cloud, making her squint. She didn't see Finch or Linnet anywhere. She hoped Linnet had found a better place for drawing.

"Where do you go on your walks?"

Eider turned to find Finch, who was shuffling his feet.

"My walks?" she repeated, playing dumb.

"Like . . . where do you go, specifically? When you leave the—"

"Shhh." Eider grabbed Finch by his bony elbow and tugged him down the slope, toward the date grove. "I didn't know you knew about those."

"Where else would you find things? And anyway, one time I saw you leave."

She paused to stare at him. "You did? Did anyone else see?"

Finch shook his head.

"Okay. Well, I don't go very far. Just along the edge of the ranch, mostly. In back, where nobody ever goes. There are ravines and stuff—"

"Can I go with you?"

For a moment, Eider was speechless. Finch, go exploring with her? She'd never even considered it. Sure, Finch was curious, but he always did what Teacher said. And besides that, he was so scared of the world Beyond—he didn't even like visiting the slabs, or standing on the rise and looking out. "Now?" she said.

"It's a good time. Everybody's busy."

That was true. But Eider didn't really feel like exploring. "You can go by yourself, you know," she said. "I don't need to go with you."

"I don't know how."

"I'll take you to the gap in the fence, okay?"

Finch shuffled his feet. "I don't know how," he said again.

Eider sighed. "Gosh, you're hopeless. Come on, let's go."

——

"Just duck your head," Eider ordered from Beyond. "Make yourself really small, and take a big step. Don't let your overalls get snagged on the fence. . . ."

Finch just stood there, staring at Eider through the gap. "You sure it's okay?"

"The hardest part is the first step. But it's still just a normal step. Except there's a fence in between."

"The hardest part is the first step," Finch repeated. He paused a moment longer, then ducked his head and squeezed through the gap. "Nothing happened."

Eider laughed. "What'd you expect? Explosions and shooting stars? For such a smart guy, you're acting pretty silly."

He reddened. "What, you weren't nervous the first time you left?"

"Of course, but I was with—" Eider stopped. "Forget it.

This is the direction I usually go. There's a bunch of metal garbage I'm sure you'll find fascinating."

Unexpectedly, Eider discovered she liked having a companion to break up the desert silence. Finch in particular, with his head full of facts. Even though they'd read all the same books, he knew so much more. Like the names of the plants Eider stepped right over.

"Creosote," he pointed out. "Prickly pear. And that's sage."

"I know sage." Eider plucked a leaf, then crushed it. "See, you can rub it between your fingers and it smells good. Robin used to like to . . ."

They were both quiet for a moment. Eider stole a glance at Finch, who was staring at the ground very intently.

She cleared her throat. "I—"

"This is cool!" Finch exclaimed, picking up a spotted gray stone. "We'll get to Rocks sometime this month. Then we'll know what all these are. Of course, we learned about some of them last year, in Geology."

Eider's lonely feeling intensified. She took a few steps, then paused. Something angular was sticking out of the dirt.

She knelt and pried it out. It was a fragment of ceramic, like the mugs they drank from during meals. But those mugs were plain white. This shard was colorful: one side pinkish orange, the other smooth and glossy, painted white with cheery blue flowers.

"It's so pretty," she said.

Finch looked at it. "But it's not useful."

"Does everything need to be?"

He shrugged.

Eider decided to keep the shard. Maybe she'd give it to Avis. Her best friend definitely preferred pretty over useful.

"Oh, hey!" Finch exclaimed. "Isn't that a motherboard?"

"A mother *what*?"

"A motherboard." He picked up something square and green. "See? These helped control computers, Before. They carried information via electricity. And ones and zeroes. Isn't that amazing?"

Ones and zeroes? Sometimes Eider had no idea what Finch was talking about. "Yeah, wow."

"So neat." He replaced it on the ground where he'd found it.

"You're not going to keep it?"

"No. I don't have any use for it."

"What exactly *are* you looking for?" Eider asked as they wandered on.

Finch shrugged his skinny shoulders. "Oh, nothing."

But as they finished their walk, Eider noticed he was even quieter than usual. And when they squeezed through the fence, he seemed less relieved to return to safety of the desert ranch than she'd expected.

"I guess it's dinnertime," Finch said, once they'd stepped inside the date grove. "Thanks for taking me." He started to walk away.

"Hey, Finch," Eider said.

He turned slowly, his face scrunched up. "Yeah?"

"You never told me why you wanted to go exploring. . . ." She was struck by a sudden thought. "It has to do with the missing pages in World Book Q–R, doesn't it? What was missing? What did you want to read about?"

Finch hesitated, as if trying to make a decision.

"When it's ready," he said, "I'll tell you."

10

SOMETHING SPECIAL

EIDER HAD NEVER THOUGHT FINCH COULD SURPRISE HER.

But when she thought about it, he was probably the second-most curious kid at the desert ranch. His curiosity was just a different kind than hers. The tinkering kind. The kind that drove him to build things, figure them out. To make things.

Eider was pretty sure Finch was making something.

And it probably wasn't a tuba.

She wanted to ask him for more details, but ears were everywhere. Linnet, trailing a few yards behind her. Jay, endlessly mocking and bellowing. Avis, who could never stand being left out.

"Are you following him to the outhouse?" she said, as Eider tried to catch up with Finch after breakfast. "Ew!"

"What?" Eider said. "No. Don't be weird."

"You're the weird one." Avis bumped Eider with her hip. "Come on, your braid's all lumpy. Let me fix it."

During Practical, Eider kept trying to catch Finch's eye. But he never looked up from his notebook. She couldn't tell if it was Finch's usual awkwardness, or if he was deliberately avoiding her gaze.

"I asked you a question," Teacher said. "Are you paying attention? Eider?"

Eider jolted. "I'm sorry. Did you ask a question?"

The other kids tittered. Teacher sighed.

"I was hoping we'd get to another Extrasensory lesson today, but it seems like someone isn't ready." She frowned at Eider. "Are you sure you've fully recovered from your spell the other day?"

Everybody groaned except Eider, who squirmed with embarrassment. She'd hoped they'd all forgotten. "I'm fine," she said. "I'm ready. I promise I'm ready."

"You're sure?"

Eider nodded adamantly.

"Okay," Teacher said. "Then we'll meet in the Circle Time area after lunch. I have very high hopes for today's lesson."

—

For their third Extrasensory lesson, Teacher divided the kids into pairs. Eider and Avis. Jay and Linnet. Finch and Teacher. "Just for the first round," she said.

Then she handed out a stack of cards. They were stiff, like Eider's desert-flower postcard. Teacher had written a simple noun on each one:

TREE
STAR
APPLE

"Take turns picking a card from the stack," Teacher said. "Keep the word a secret. But picture it in your head, as clearly as you can. Your partner will try to guess it."

"Like . . . reading each other's minds?" Avis asked.

Eider raised her eyebrows. Mind reading seemed awfully far-fetched for a lesson, even an Extrasensory one.

Though if anybody could read minds, it would have been Robin. In Eider's memories-that-weren't, she always seemed to know what Eider was thinking or feeling. Sometimes Eider would catch Robin gazing at her, and she'd picture something ridiculous, on purpose. Like a monkey or—or a pineapple. And then Robin would grin, like she knew exactly what Eider was trying to do.

Which made sense, since Eider was Robin and Robin was Eider.

"Not mind reading, necessarily," Teacher replied. "It's more like sharing. Sharing words. Here at the desert ranch, you're all connected. I want to test how connected you are."

Far-fetched or not, it sounded fun at first. But after just a handful of cards, it was clear: Everybody was *terrible*.

Even after they swapped partners. Eider and Linnet. Eider and Jay—yuck. And then Eider and Avis again, who was having trouble keeping the whine from her voice.

"Giraffe?" Avis asked. "Potato?"

"Nope." Eider concentrated so hard she felt her forehead crumple.

"Just tell me."

Eider showed Avis the card:

BANANA

Avis snorted. "Not even close."

"Well . . . bananas are long, like a giraffe's neck. And yellow. Maybe you got some of that?"

"But my other guess was a potato. What does that have to do with a banana?"

Eider didn't know. "They're both food?"

"This is stupid," Avis said. "Why would I *want* anybody to be able to read my mind anyway? Do you really want Jay to know what we're thinking?"

Eider glanced at Jay, who was making fish faces at Finch.

"Good point," she said.

Avis scowled. "It's creepy."

Eider hoped Teacher hadn't heard. She knew Avis was just feeling frustrated again—she hated it when she wasn't good at something. Even more than she hated being left out.

Although in this case, none of the kids was a natural. At the end of the lesson, Teacher accepted the stacks of cards and wound rubber bands around them with a *smack*. At least her disappointment wasn't aimed at just Eider this time.

"We'll have to try again," she said. *Smack*. "You know I have faith in you—but faith only goes so far. You'll need to try harder. Much harder." *Smack*.

Beside Eider, Avis exhaled audibly.

Teacher raised her eyebrows. "Is anything wrong, Avis?"

"Well . . ." Avis said. "No. But I was wondering. What if—what if we'll never be any good at this?"

"Maybe you aren't good at it now. But you will be."

"But what if we just . . . *can't*?"

"That's not possible."

There was an unmistakable warning in Teacher's voice now. Luckily, Avis knew when to shut up.

"And here's why," Teacher went on. "Brains are like wads of clay. They can become almost anything with the right pinching and prodding. But they're not stuck that way. You can squash them and start all over again; remold them into something different. Something more.

"It helps to start out as a natural, of course. But with you kids, it shouldn't matter. As I've told you time and again, your brains are the best and the brightest of all. With the most potential—if you're willing to make the effort.

"In other words," she finished, "you're just not trying hard enough."

—

That evening, Eider was first back to their trailer. She couldn't get Teacher's words out of her head. If brains could be pinched and prodded into anything, why couldn't she stop thinking about Robin? Because she wasn't trying hard enough?

She sure felt like she was trying. But her thoughts constantly caught her off guard, especially when her real memories overlapped with memories-that-weren't. Partial truths, partial stories. Confusing her reality.

"What's that?" Linnet asked. It came out in a squeaky burst, like she'd done everything she could to prevent the question from escaping.

Instead of her penlight, Eider realized she'd pulled out the ceramic shard—the one she'd found while exploring with Finch. She really needed to do a better job emptying her pockets. "Just something I found," she said.

"Can—can I see?" Linnet asked.

Eider hesitated a second. It wasn't anything that would get her in trouble, she reasoned. Just a piece of junk, not anything off-limits or useful. She handed it over.

Linnet held it gingerly in the center of her palm, as if she was afraid she might break it. "Are those flowers?"

"I think so."

"I've never seen blue flowers before. Most flowers in real life are yellow, you know? Like the mesquite ones, and the cactus ones. What do you think it belonged to?"

Eider smiled. She'd never heard Linnet talk this much. "A mug, maybe? Or a bowl?"

"That's neat." Linnet reached out to return the shard—but hesitantly, like she didn't want to let it go.

"Do you want to keep it?" Eider asked.

"Really?" It came out as a higher-pitched squeak than ever. "Oh, but—are you sure? It's so special."

Eider wondered why Linnet was making such a big deal about it. The shard was pretty, but it wasn't useful. Finch had been right about that. "Sure! I find lots of stuff. Maybe you can draw it?"

"Oh, no, I . . ." Linnet touched the painted side, stroking the tiny flowers. "Thank you."

Eider nodded. "Sure."

Just a piece of junk, not anything useful. But at breakfast the next morning, Eider saw Linnet's fingers moving in her side pocket. As if she had something special hidden there.

11

ALL THAT WORLD

THE FOLLOWING NIGHT, Eider fell asleep early and dreamed of cement ships riding huge, crashing waves. Except the sea stank of dead fish. And it was wrong-colored. She knew she had to find the real sea, the blue one with the mermaids, but she had no way of steering. She was stuck going wherever the waves wanted to take her.

"*Eider.*"

Her eyes shot open. The trailer was dark. She squinted and scanned it, but only saw Linnet and Avis, asleep in their beds.

"*Eider!*"

The second hiss made her sit up. Then she saw Finch's pale face squished against the trailer's window. She pushed back her sheets and opened the trailer door a crack.

"What are you doing here?" she whispered. "You're messing up my circadian rhythms."

"I've finished the radio," he said.

"The what?"

"The radio. I built one."

Eider paused as his words sank in. Then a jolt of excitement tightened her chest.

Finch continued, "If you want to come with me, I'll show you."

A real-life radio? Of course she wanted to see it! But she didn't want to get in trouble. "Is anybody awake?"

"I saw the light in Teacher's trailer. And I waited for it to turn off."

Eider hesitated only a second longer. If anybody could bring to life something he'd only read about, it was Finch. "Okay. Let me get my boots."

"What's going on?"

It was Avis, sitting up in her bed. Linnet slept on.

"Nothing," Eider said.

"Doesn't look like nothing. Tell me."

"I don't think you'd want to—" Eider whispered.

"How do you know what I want? Whatever you're doing, I'm coming along."

Eider sighed. Avis never wanted to talk about Beyond. She barely even seemed to wonder about it. Eider doubted she'd be interested in a radio, let alone approve of one.

But then again, she was Eider's best friend. She'd always kept Eider's secrets—about the fairytale book, her explorations, and more. And, anyway, Eider knew from experience Avis wouldn't let this go.

"Do you mind?" Eider asked Finch.

He shrugged his bony shoulders. "Fine."

—

Eider had never thought much about radios.

She'd been interested in music, though. Music, and dancing. She even remembered the Circle Time when it all began, years ago.

"Before," Teacher had told them, "there were objects called radios that captured music sent from other places. The music was played with musical instruments: drums, banjos, pianos, guitars. And the instrument of one's voice."

She'd hummed music, low and sweet. Teacher's voice was formal, usually, but the humming had been beautiful.

"Did you dance to the music?" Eider remembered asking.

Teacher hadn't waved away as many questions back then. "Everybody danced Before," she replied. "Dancing is just moving one's body to the beat of music. Anything from slow swaying to stylized dances, like tap or ballet." For a moment, she'd closed her eyes. "We loved ballet the most."

Eider hadn't known who *we* meant—probably Teacher and Nurse, although the idea of Nurse dancing made her snort.

But after that, Eider had been obsessed with ballet. She'd memorized the poses described in a book and practiced them over and over. She'd had no way of knowing whether they were right. But they'd *felt* right.

One day, Teacher had pulled Eider aside. "You've been working very hard," she'd said. "I have a reward for you."

She'd pulled out a pair of ballet slippers, the pale pink color of a kit fox's tongue.

"Now you'll be able to dance better. Even if you're not able to dance on your toes like a proper ballerina."

Breathlessly, Eider had accepted the slippers. They'd been in remarkably good condition, with only a few scuffed patches. She remembered wondering who they had belonged to Before.

She also remembered refusing to let Robin wear them.

"They're way too big for you. You'll trip and fall flat on your face. And break your nose. And then you won't be able to smell anymore."

"I don't care about smelling."

"Obviously. Because you stink!"

Shrieking with laughter, Robin had chased Eider under the twin windmills, then all the way up the rise. The ballet slippers had ended up even more scuffed, but Eider hadn't really cared.

Atop the rise, they'd danced together, their arms reaching toward the sky. They hummed the same music, low and sweet, their voices blending as one.

———

Could Finch's radio capture music?

Eider was dying to find out. But she had to walk slowly, since Avis was latched onto her arm. During Physical, Avis was the most agile. But at night she kept losing her footing on the uneven ground. She didn't have much experience venturing off the desert ranch's same old paths, like Eider did.

"This better be worth it," Avis said, aiming her penlight at Eider. "What's the deal, anyway?"

"Turn that off! You'll see when we get there."

"I didn't even fix my hair. Also, it's freezing out. Why didn't you make me bring my jacket?"

"I never said not to," Eider said.

"But you should have told me. . . ."

As they approached the cement slabs, Eider couldn't help thinking of her dream ship and the dead-fish sea. When she inhaled, she could almost smell it. She rubbed her nose.

Finch was there already, his radio sitting beside him. Or what Eider assumed was his radio. It looked like a small heap of metal parts, barely connected. She tried not to reveal how disappointed she felt.

Avis wrinkled her nose. "What's that, a broken robot?"

"It's a radio," Finch said.

"Obviously," Eider said, even though it wasn't obvious at all. "How did you know how to build it without the Radio section, Finch?"

"From memory, mostly," he replied. "We used to have a book called *The Way Things Work*. Then I found stuff about batteries in World Book B, and circuits in World Book C. The rest was trial and error—"

"Yeah, yeah, we know you're a genius," Avis said.

"How does it work?" Eider asked.

"Well, the receiver collects electromagnetic energy—"

"Not in Finchspeak!" Avis protested. "Talk like a normal person."

Finch huffed. "*Fine*. Radios capture sound waves in the air that are broadcasted—sent—from other places. So people can listen to things from far away. Like music. And news reports."

"News reports?" Eider repeated. She'd only thought about music. But news reports sounded just as intriguing.

"About what's going on in the world. People could sit in their homes and learn about everything going on, all over the—"

"*Before*," Avis said, jumping in. "People could, *Before*. Nobody's out there sending anything now."

"Do we know that for sure?" Finch said.

Eider stared at Finch, a strange feeling in her middle. She wished she'd been able to talk about this without Avis around. "Do you really think there might be something out there?"

Finch nodded. "I do."

"What?" Avis scoffed. "Come on, you guys! That's silly. We know there's nothing left. Nothing and nobody."

"I think what's silly is assuming we're the only ones left," he said. "Do you know how big the world is?"

"Sure. It's big. So?"

"I mean, do you *really* know? Have you done the math?" Finch's eyes, typically squinty blue, seemed to double in size. "Have you ever pictured how big a foot is? Or a hundred feet? How about five thousand of them, to make a mile? Do you know how big a mile is?"

Eider nodded.

Finch glanced at her, then went on. "The world is thousands of miles around. Imagine all that world. Somebody else *has* to be out there. Maybe lots of somebodies."

"Cities!" Eider said breathlessly.

"Other People, at least." Finch paused. "But whether they're broadcasting anything is another story."

"But if they are . . ."

"If they are, and they're not *too* far away . . . I think my radio will capture it."

Eider's strange feeling blossomed into flower. She sat beside Finch on the cement slab. "Then what are we waiting for? Let's turn it on!"

Avis remained standing. "You *guys*," she said again, shaking her head. Her braids wriggled like rust-colored snakes.

"I think I've almost got it," Finch said.

He wiggled a wire. Poked at it. Swiveled a dial. Then all three of them leaned in involuntarily—Avis, too—as the first tinny hum shivered through the speaker. The only sound in that desert night.

"Do you hear it?" Finch broke into a grin.

Eider and Avis couldn't help grinning, too. "It's working!" Eider exclaimed.

"Is it?" Avis said.

"Yeah, obviously!"

"But it's only, like . . . buzzing."

They listened harder. Avis was right—all they heard was an electric crackle. It was a stormy sound, like wind and rain tickling the desert floor. From time to time, there was a sharp, low *pop*, but that was it. No voices. No music.

"Hold on . . ." Finch said.

He swiveled the dial again. Back and forth. Slowly, then more quickly as his frustration seemed to increase. The sounds didn't change: nothing but the same dull hum.

"I'll keep working on it," Finch promised. "Maybe I just need a different battery. Or a better wire. If there's anything out there, we'll hear it."

Unless there's nothing out there after all, Eider thought but didn't say. She didn't need to. They were all thinking the same thing.

12

WAR GAMES

"VERY GOOD," TEACHER SAID TO LINNET, who'd just finished reading the Racing section in World Book R. On the wall behind her, the cardboard names still hung in yesterday's arrangement:

FINCH
JAY   EIDER   LINNET
AVIS

Eider figured it meant some of the kids were tied. But she didn't want to ask, since it might draw attention to Avis—ranked last, for the second time.

"That's about all the time we have," Teacher said. "I need to take care of some important work in my office."

Jay raised his hand. "Free Play?"

She nodded. "I think so. It's cooler today—how about you all play together outside?"

The kids knew better than to groan audibly, but Eider suspected they all were groaning inwardly. Even before the rankings, they'd always had trouble agreeing on a group activity. Jay would want to play something rough-and-tumble. Avis would tell everyone what to do. And so on.

Obediently, the kids filed outside and crowded into the shade under a mesquite tree. "Anybody have any ideas?" Avis asked. "How about follow the leader?"

"Who's that, you?" Jay said.

Avis's cheeks went pink. "Not necessarily."

"Hopscotch?" Linnet suggested, doodling in the dirt with the toe of her boot. When she saw Eider watching, she stopped.

"Or four square," Jay said.

"Four square is boring," Avis said.

"You're boring."

Avis kicked a pebble at him.

Same old bickering, Eider thought. Same old everything. Without even the hope of Finch's radio to break it up. She wished she could hide in the storage room and reread her fairytale book. Sometimes, there was nothing like a good story to—

"Bang!" Jay yelled in her ear.

Eider yelped. "What the heck, Jay?"

He clasped his hands together with his index fingers

pointing out, aiming them her way. "Bang! Bang!"

"Are you being a gun?" Avis asked, eyes narrowed.

"I'm not a gun," Jay explained. "I'm a soldier holding one."

"That's nothing. Dream bigger." Avis slung back her arm and aimed at Finch. "Laser gun! Zap, zap, *explode*!"

Involuntarily, Finch covered his head. Eider couldn't help laughing. "What in the world is a laser gun?" she asked Avis.

"It's for shooting lasers, obviously."

Eider had no idea where Avis had gotten that from. One of the old books, maybe? The Guns section has been missing from World Book G. And they hadn't gotten to World Book S yet, for Soldiers, or World Book W, for War—which it seemed like they were playing. She wasn't sure how she felt about that. Teacher had always said war was very serious, after all.

"Luckily, I've got one for you too," Avis said. "Catch!"

Avis pretended to throw a laser gun at Eider. Eider sighed and pretended to catch it, staggering under its imaginary weight.

"Bang!" Jay yelled. "Hey Linnet, get out your rifles already! They're strapped to your back."

"I have more than one?" she asked.

"The other one's for Finch." He jumped from the slab boat. "I hear horses—the cavalry is coming! Run!"

All five of them ran, their boots crunching through

the brown-baked sage. They hadn't played pretend games together in a long while. Maybe they'd each suspected the others had outgrown them.

"Spaceships overhead!" Avis yelled. "Duck!"

"From what?" Finch asked.

"Bombs, obviously."

"You can't duck from a bomb."

"Well duh, not if it falls straight on you. But if it falls nearby, you should duck to avoid the things, the pieces—"

"The shrapnel," Finch said.

"You should duck to avoid the shrapnel."

"That wouldn't do any good either. Shrapnel is like bullets. That's why soldiers hid in trenches."

"Is a trench like a ravine?" Linnet asked. "We have lots of those."

"Jay!" Eider called. "Don't just jump in there, you've got to check for rattlesnakes first. Seriously—"

"Zap!" Avis exclaimed in her ear.

Eider pushed her away, laughing. "You're my best friend! Aren't you on my side?"

"You're no good to me if you're not paying attention. Look, Jay's back is turned. Let's blow him into hyperspace."

They ran at him, hollering wildly, imaginary laser guns blasting potholes into the sand. Eider lost all track of time. She'd always pictured war as a scary thing. But it was also a game, wasn't it? Or at least a kind of sport. Strategy, planning, running, playing.

Then Jay's boot came down on the wrong kind of earth and he slipped, skidding a few feet on the seat of his pants. Avis shrieked in laughter, dodging the dirt clod Jay threw.

"You tripped me!" he yelled, lumbering to his feet.

"Oh, she did not," Eider said.

Jay turned his red-cheeked glare her way. "How would you know, cloudface? Your brain's totally M.I.A."

"Your *face* is totally—" Avis began. "Wait, what does M.I.A. mean?"

"Missing in action," Jay said. "Like when a soldier runs off and abandons his platoon. And nobody ever finds him again. You know, like Robin."

Eider froze.

"Jay!" Avis punched him in the arm. Hard. "What's wrong with you? Shut your oaf mouth."

"Did he say—"

"Nothing. Don't listen. He's just being mean." Avis tugged on Eider's elbow, pulling her away.

"But he said she ran off." Tears pricked at Eider's eyes. "That's what—"

"It's just a game, Eider. And obviously Jay knows he's not supposed to bring up— He's just a jerk. We should tell Teacher on him. Come on."

"Wait . . ."

But Avis was already running. They hadn't gotten far when she stumbled to a stop. Eider nearly crashed into her back.

"I'm not sure we should—" Eider began, but Avis's expression interrupted her. She followed her gaze to the top of the rise, where Teacher stood.

Arms crossed. Shoulders tense. Mouth firm.

Eider's stomach dropped. How long had Teacher been watching? She'd seen them pretending to shoot each other, duck from bombs, fall down dead. War was very serious, and the kids had made it a game. All thoughts of telling on Jay scattered in the face of Teacher's disappointment.

"Uh-oh," Avis said under her breath.

As the kids trudged up the rise to join her, Teacher remained where she stood. She looked more than disappointed. She looked betrayed.

"We're sorry," Eider blurted. "We were only—"

Before she could finish, Teacher turned and walked away.

———

Teacher didn't like to talk about how the world had ended.

"It doesn't matter anymore," she'd said time and again. "The important parts are what happened Before and After. Not what happened in between."

She'd told them a little, of course. Even if they hadn't gotten to World Book W yet, they knew about wars from the old books. Civil. I and II. There'd even been a book about the star's wars, fought in outer spaces.

Teacher claimed the end of the world had been different, though. It hadn't ended in any big, scary way. Just a long, slow taper. Everything growing worse and worse until, suddenly, it was all gone.

"Poof," Jay had shouted.

The kids had been much younger then. But even though the topic was scary, they'd all stifled a giggle. Just to think that everything they'd heard about and read about—narwhals and puffins and great white sharks, music and automobiles, soaring gold-colored bridges and buildings that scraped the sky—all those amazing things had just disappeared with a *poof*! Like a magic trick.

"But why?" Eider remembered asking. "Why did it all go away?"

"Because the world was going rotten," Teacher had explained. "Too many people were born with ill in their hearts. Like a sickness, they spread it. Until the good people were outnumbered by billons. The world *had* to end—there was no other choice."

"But it didn't end for everyone," Avis had said.

"No, not for everyone," Teacher had agreed. "Not for you."

She'd smiled at them, kid by kid, around the entire table.

"You children are brilliant and special and purehearted. That's why you're here right now. You are better. You are *more*. You are truly good."

Hearing that had usually made Eider feel proud. But

that time, she'd squinted a bit. Jay, truly good? She'd just seen him push Finch into a tumbleweed that morning. And Eider had laughed, which meant she wasn't all that pure-hearted herself.

"What happened to Other People?" Eider had asked.

"What do you mean?" Teacher had replied.

"All the people besides us. When the world ended, what happened to them?"

Teacher's smile had faded. "It doesn't matter," she'd said, waving her hand. "They're not here anymore. Which means—it means they're not anything we should worry about. They're not suffering in the world as it is now.

"You're the luckiest children in the world," Teacher reminded them. "You have everything you need. You're safe and surrounded by people who care about you. You get to live out your lives. You *exist*."

Eider did feel lucky.

Everywhere else, the world had ended. But at the desert ranch, it went on. That was the important part, even if there weren't any automobiles or circuses or pumpkin coaches. At the desert ranch, the world still existed.

And so did they.

Eider thought Teacher might scold them about the war games, but she didn't.

In fact, she spoke very little. During Practical, she had the kids read section after section, with none of her usual discussion. She just watched them perplexedly, like she'd realized she didn't know them at all.

Her mood affected everyone. After Physical, which they'd spent running around the fence, Eider overheard Nurse ask Teacher if everything was okay.

"Not if you keep asking ridiculous questions," Teacher snapped back.

By dinnertime (canned sausages, rice, and stewed tomatoes, yuck), Teacher was already in her office. The kids ate in quiet discomfort, clearing their plates even though they knew she wouldn't check.

"Quiet Time for the rest of the evening," Nurse said, with none of his usual loopiness. In fact, his face resembled the mean dog's, right after the Handyman yelled.

Everything felt wrong. And it was all Jay's fault.

Maybe not entirely, but mostly. Playing war had been his idea. And what was more, he'd brought up Robin, when he knew he wasn't supposed to. Stupid, buffalo-brained Jay, whom Eider had never liked or trusted.

She couldn't let him get away with it.

—

Eider waited for the other kids to disperse. Just like she expected, Jay disappeared into his trailer, then reappeared with a box.

She followed him.

Unlike Eider's secret papers and Avis's scraps and Finch's odds and ends, Jay's collection was creepy. Freaky, even. Eider watched him open the box and place each item on the ground behind his trailer.

The skull of a coyote.

Snail shells with the snails missing.

A crispy, withered rattlesnake skin.

A rattlesnake rattle.

Worst of all, an entire board of bugs with nails through them. Moths with their wings spread. Shiny black stink-bugs. Right in the center, a wicked-looking scorpion. Eider hated scorpions almost as much as rattlesnakes. Jay must have caught the bugs, stabbed them, and mounted them so he could—well, do whatever he did with his dead things.

As Eider approached him, she felt nervous, but she knew she couldn't show it. She plunked her hands on her hips and used her most overbearing, Avis-like voice.

"Hey there, oaf! Nice collection."

"What are you doing here?" Instantly, Jay started putting his creatures back inside the box. His big hands fumbled, knocking over the coyote skull.

"You made Teacher upset with us," Eider said. "You and your stupid war games."

"Me? You all played, too!"

"Yeah, but you started it." She took a deep breath. "And—and why'd you bring up—why'd you . . ."

"Spit it out, cloudface."

After so much time swallowing her sister's name, Eider discovered her mouth refused to form it. "You know what I'm talking about."

"*You know what I'm talking about,*" Jay mimicked.

Eider scowled. Avis had been right—Jay was just a jerk. "Why are you so mean all the time?" she demanded. "No wonder nobody trusts you."

"So what?" He replaced the lid on his box. "It's not like I trust you either."

"*You* don't trust *me*?" Even though it was only Jay, Eider felt extremely offended. "Why not?"

"You're always up to something. You're sneaky."

"I'm not sneaky!"

"Yes, you are. Or you *think* you are, but you're not. All that stuff you're up to, it's obvious. Maybe not to Teacher, but to the rest of us."

Eider didn't know what to say. Because it was true, of course. She was always sneaking around—to the slabs, the storage room, through the gap in the fence. She'd thought she'd been getting away with it, but the other kids had noticed.

How long before Teacher noticed, too?

Eider cleared her throat. "Well, I'm not the only one sneaking around. Why would anyone collect dead things? Like that board of stabbed bugs—did you kill them yourself?"

"What?" Jay looked gravely insulted. "I didn't kill them!"

"Then who did?"

"They died of natural causes! However things die normally—I just found them. I pinned them to the board so I could see them better."

Eider wrinkled her nose. "Why do you want to see them?"

"Because they're interesting."

"How are dead bugs interesting? They're disgusting."

"No, they're not," Jay insisted. "I like looking at their wings and exoskeletons. Seeing how they fit together."

"Why don't you look at them when they're alive?"

"I try when I can. But how am I supposed to get a good look at a rattlesnake when it's alive? Or a scorpion? Or a stinkbug? Even moths and beetles won't sit still."

"It's still weird."

Jay looked exasperated. "Just because something's not interesting to you doesn't mean it's not interesting to someone else."

Eider remembered how Avis rolled her eyes when she spoke about the sea. Or how Eider never understood Finch's odds and ends, his metal scraps and snarls of wires. Until he turned them into a radio—*then* she was interested. She shook her head, feeling a little ashamed. Jay was wiser than his dopey tree-trunk voice suggested.

"I guess that makes sense," Eider said. "Sorry I was mean about your collection."

Jay frowned at her, like an apology was the last thing he expected. Then he shrugged his brawny shoulders. "It's all right, cloudface. I'm sorry. . . ." He waved his hand dismissively, like Teacher did. But it was good enough for Eider.

"Why do you hide your collection, anyway?" she asked. "If it's only for studying?"

He stared a moment longer, like he didn't have a good answer. Then he picked up his box and hurried away.

———

During Quiet Time, Eider hovered outside the storage room. She couldn't make up her mind whether to go inside.

Then a poke between her wingbones made her jump. She turned to find Finch, looking more animated than usual.

"I'm ready to try again," he said. "I found another battery. I think it might be the solution."

"You found a battery? Where?"

"In that same ravine we explored before. I went during Quiet Time yesterday."

Eider's jaw dropped. "You went exploring by yourself?"

Finch wrinkled his nose. "I didn't go very far. Can we meet this evening? At the slabs?"

Eider was all set to say yes, but then she hesitated. *You're always up to something*, Jay had said. *You're sneaky.* The same reason she hadn't entered the storage room yet.

But what if the radio did work? And she wasn't there to hear it? Eider had read the phrase "partners in crime" in a book long ago, and she finally understood it. At least if she and Finch got in trouble, they'd get in trouble together.

"Of course," she said.

Finch grinned. "If possible, could you try to come without waking . . ." He didn't finish his sentence, but Eider knew what he meant.

"Just me," she said.

The crunch of footsteps interrupted them. "Oh,

whoopsie!" Nurse said. "What are you two doing over here?"

Eider was glad they were standing outside the storage room, not in it. "Studying," she said breezily. An excuse that always worked with Nurse. "Finch had a bunch of questions about today's lesson."

"I did not," Finch said.

Eider kicked him in the ankle.

"Studying! That's what Teacher and I like to hear. Much better than pickle stealing, am I right?"

"Pickle stealing?" Finch repeated.

Nurse tweaked Finch's nose. "This is no place to study, anyhow. How about I walk you back to your trailers?"

"Sure," Eider said.

"I don't even *like* pickles," Finch muttered.

—

That night, Eider waited until the other girls' breathing was even. Then she pulled on her boots, tiptoed down the trailer steps, and crept into the night.

A slight breeze disrupted the dark—not really strong enough for papers to come, although you never knew. But its electric whisper made the desert feel alive. Like anything could happen. Like maybe there really was music in the air. Or voices from Beyond, just waiting to be captured by Finch's radio.

A light was on in Teacher's office, but Eider couldn't see into it. None of the kids had ever been inside. As if the rusty old sign in front of the spike applied to it, too.

NO TRESPASSING
KEEP OUT

None of the kids had been inside Teacher's trailer, either. One evening, though, Eider had seen Teacher standing at its window. She'd been lantern-lit from behind, gazing out at the desert. Her long, white hair had hung loose. As Eider had watched, she'd gathered it over one shoulder and run a brush through it, again and again. But her eyes had been the strangest part: they'd looked so *sad*.

The memory still made Eider feel funny. It was the most human Teacher had ever seemed.

Finch was already waiting at the cement slabs. He wore his jacket over his nightshirt, the hood pulled over his head. The radio sat beside him. If he'd swapped one of the wires, Eider couldn't tell.

"Have you tried it yet?" Eider asked, sitting on the other side of the radio.

Finch's hood fell off as he nodded. "I heard something."

"You . . ." She paused to take a deeper breath. Somewhere, a night bird cried out. "What did you hear?"

"I'm not sure—I turned it off."

"Why in the world did you do that?"

"I got nervous."

Eider laughed. "Finch, you're so weird! Why did you get nervous?"

"Because . . . what if I was wrong? What if it doesn't work?" Finch paused. "Or what if . . . what if it *does*?"

They sat with that thought for a silent moment.

"Let's do it," Eider said. She had an urge to take Finch's hand. That was what she would have done if it were Avis. But Finch wasn't her best friend.

He reached for the tiny knob. Touched two wires together. The same crackly sound whispered through the speakers. "I know I heard something," he said. "I *know* it."

He kept messing with it, wiggling the wires, tapping the knob ever so gently. Eider listened hard. And then— almost imperceptibly at first—the crackly hum sharpened. Clarified. Into what sounded like . . . a *voice*.

A voice!

A real, live human voice.

Eider pressed her knuckles against her mouth with one hand, then grabbed Finch's arm with the other. She could hardly believe it. She couldn't believe it! Definitely a voice. Not singing, but talking. A talking voice—broadcast from Beyond.

But . . . the voice was grainy. A voice with ants running through it. Impossible to understand.

"This is so frustrating!" Eider exclaimed.

"That almost sounded like—" Finch began. "No, maybe not."

Unable to hold back any longer, Eider reached out and tapped the knob herself. Immediately, the voice sharpened.

"There it is!" Finch whispered. "Listen!"

Heart racing, Eider closed her eyes and listened as hard as she could. Sifting through the sound, like she had during their first Extrasensory lesson. Bundling it in her clenched fists. Then her eyes flew open.

"*Storm*," she said.

"Storm?" Finch repeated.

Eider nodded, her insides flip-flopping. "I heard it. I heard the word *storm*."

"Are you sure? I think it sounded more like *warm*. Or *worm*."

"Why would it be *worm*?"

"Why would it be *storm*? It barely ever rains here."

She rolled her eyes. "Let's keep listening."

But no matter how much they jostled the knob and wires, they couldn't make out any other words. Before long, the voice died out. All that remained was that hushed, frustrating crackle.

They'd captured just the smallest windblown scrap of a story. A World Book with just one page left: Storm. (Because it *definitely* wasn't *worm*.)

But it was enough. For now, anyway.

Because the most important message of all came

through loud and clear. Not only were there Other People still out there, after the end of the world—but there were people broadcasting.

People who wanted to be heard.

OTHER PEOPLE

EIDER WALKED BACK TO HER TRAILER IN A DAZE. Before she'd even shut the door, Avis asked, "Where'd you go?"

"To the outhouse," Eider whispered, kicking off her boots and climbing into bed.

"Yeah, right. You were gone too long for that."

"I got a drink of water, too."

Linnet's bed creaked. "What's going on?" she asked.

"Nothing," Eider told her. "Everybody go to sleep."

Avis didn't say anything.

Eider knew she should feel sorry for leaving her out. Especially after she'd defended Eider during the war games. But right now, Eider's emotions were too preoccupied. Whirling, spinning, spiraling like a dust devil in her chest.

Other People.

Those two words echoed in Eider's head all night. And

all morning. With every footstep in the crunchy desert dirt. With every clink of her spoon in her oatmeal bowl. With every meaningful glance from Finch, until she told him to quit it.

Other People, Eider thought as she waited her turn at the obstacle course. During her checkup with Nurse. As Avis read the Railroads section in World Book Q–R with a yawn in her voice.

It was like Finch had said. The world was big. *Huge!* Once upon a time, Eider had walked forever and hadn't gotten far at all. In all that vastness, of course there were others. Others who looked outward, the same way she did. Others with the kinds of radios that broadcasted.

What if Finch could make one of those next?

The idea was exhilarating—and terrifying. If Eider could speak to Other People, what would she say? She didn't have a message for anyone. Only questions—so many questions. Questions she'd wanted to ask Teacher, but hadn't been able to.

One question stood out the most:

Do you know about the Other People?

And if Teacher did know, had known this whole time . . . why hadn't she told them?

As Eider watched Finch's clumsy stumble through the obstacle course, she tried to remember what Teacher *had* told them. It wasn't easy. She'd told the kids there was nobody left, though. Almost definitely.

Hadn't she?

Eider couldn't quite remember if Teacher had said it, or had only implied it. She did remember what Teacher had said about the sea.

"I just don't want you to get your hopes up, Eider. I've told you time and again, there's nothing left."

But that wasn't strictly true. Sure, there weren't mermaids or narwhals. But the sea still had water—plenty of water. Sand made of fish bones was still sand. So what *did* Teacher mean by "nothing"? Nothing good? Nothing worth seeing or talking about?

Were the Other People not worth talking about?

Eider wished she could approach Teacher the way she'd used to. When she'd asked her questions instead of stockpiled them. The rattlesnake fever had changed everything. Trying to run away had changed everything.

Back then, Eider had believed in Other People. She'd had hope—just no proof.

Now she might have actual proof. And she was more confused than ever.

———

"Today's Extrasensory lesson is about telepathy," Teacher announced. She didn't seem disappointed in the kids anymore. In fact, she seemed upbeat. Even excited.

It made Eider feel a little excited herself, which was a

relief. Her endless loop of questions was starting to strangle her brain.

Jay raised his hand. "Telepathy? Is that like telephone?"

"No, it's . . ." Teacher tapped her chin with her long fingers. "Actually, I suppose the words have the same root. They're both about sending messages from one place to another, from one person to another. Telephones, telegraphs. Even radios."

Eider felt Finch's eyes on her, but she didn't turn to look.

"But with telepathy, you'll only use your minds. Same with telekinesis. And teleportation."

Unfamiliar words, but they seemed to excite Teacher even more.

"Those lessons are far, far down the line, though," she said. "You'll have to master these easy ones first."

"*Easy?*" Avis whispered.

Teacher went on. "We used telepathy in our last Extrasensory lesson. Or tried to, anyway. I've had a few days to contemplate what went wrong, and I believe it was the cards themselves. The cards got in the way.

"This time, I want you each to think of an object. Ideally, something that evokes emotion. Don't just picture the word, but the object itself. You'll go one at a time, thinking of your object, while the other kids try their best to see what it is."

Jay was first. He stood in front of the others, his face screwed up in concentration. "Okay," he said at last.

"A rock?" Finch guessed.

"A buffalo?" Avis tried, then giggled. Teacher didn't smile.

Eider stared at Jay, trying to see his thoughts. All she saw was his unpleasant face. What would Jay be thinking about? She remembered his board of bugs with pins in them. The wicked-looking bug in the center.

"A scorpion," she said.

Jay's eyes widened. "She's right!"

Teacher smiled, and Eider smiled too. Beside her, Avis frowned.

Finch was up next. For some reason, he couldn't stop twitching: shuffling his feet, rubbing his nose. Eider wished she could telepathically tell him to relax. "He's thinking about the World Book," she guessed. "World Book Q–R, specifically."

"That's right!" Finch exclaimed, a little too loud.

"Nice job, Eider!" Teacher said. "You just might be a natural at this. How about you go next?"

Beaming, Eider took her place at the front of the group. The first object that came to mind was the housing-development pamphlet, with its pages full of families. That wouldn't work. Nor her fairytale book, which she pictured next. Then the gap in the fence. Then Finch's radio. Now she understood why he'd gotten all twitchy—she was starting to twitch too.

What else was there? Her penlight! Too obvious, but at least it wouldn't get her in trouble. "Okay," she said.

"Avis? What do you see?" Teacher asked.

"I don't know," Avis said flatly. "Oatmeal. The wash bucket. A giraffe eating a banana."

Eider laughed. "Not even close."

"I need you to take this seriously, Avis," Teacher said sharply.

Avis reddened. And then she blurted: "She's obviously just thinking about Robin."

Everybody gasped. The name hit Eider like a fist in her belly. "I wasn't!" she exclaimed. "I swear I wasn't."

The other kids looked as shocked as Eider felt. Jay being mean was nothing unusual, but Avis? In front of Teacher? Eider braced herself for a scolding. Or worse, discipline. But Teacher's glare was aimed elsewhere.

"What's gotten into you lately, Avis?"

"Into *me*? Eider's the one who—"

"I didn't say anything about Eider. It's you I'm speaking to right now. Do you have a problem with this lesson?"

The only right answer was no. But for some reason, Avis didn't say it. She stood there with her mouth twisted, her eyebrows furrowed. "I just don't—"

"Yes?"

"I just don't see why any of this is important, all right?" Avis burst out. "Extrasensory lessons are silly. They're not making us stronger or smarter. They're just make-believe. Just stupid make-believe."

Everyone stood very still. Linnet gulped audibly, then covered her mouth.

"Extrasensory lessons aren't make-believe," Teacher said. "Not only are they real, they're important. The most important lessons of all."

"Why?" Avis asked. "Why do they matter? Why does *any* of this matter?"

Eider cringed. They were questions she'd always wanted to ask—but Avis was asking all wrong. Didn't she remember what happened when Robin threw tantrums?

Of course she didn't. But Eider could.

In Eider's memories-that-weren't, Robin had thrown lots of them. Stamped her feet and stuck out her tongue and yelled at the top of her lungs. Teacher would threaten to discipline her, but she never had. . . .

Because Robin wasn't real. Eider squeezed her eyes shut, then opened them. Teacher was silent, still suspiciously calm. She looked from kid to kid: Avis to Linnet to Jay, Jay to Finch to Eider. Back to Avis, who was staring at her feet.

"I'll explain," Teacher said.

15 THE POINT

IN THE CLASSROOM, nobody knew whether to sit or stand. Jay and Linnet sat. Eider and Avis stood. Finch hovered somewhere between sitting and standing. They'd left their notebooks behind, flapping in the breeze. Maybe they'd blow away and become some other person's secret papers, Eider thought.

"There are many things we know," Teacher began. "And many things we don't. We can only do our best to guess—to make *educated* guesses, based on what we do know. Based on facts."

She nodded at the World Books, lined up on their shelves.

"The world has ended. That's a fact. It's ended—everywhere but here, at the desert ranch. Here, you're sheltered and protected. You're the most brilliant, the most special, the purehearted, the truly good.

"And you're here for a reason."

A reason? Eider made fists to avoid biting her thumbnails. She felt nervous, or maybe excited. It was hard to tell which.

"Here, at the desert ranch," Teacher said. "Here, after the end of the world. Here: where and when you exist. Right here. You know you're here to learn. But you're also here to train—for the world beginning again."

The start of everything good again. The beginning of the beginning.

It was all Eider could do not to look at Finch, or Avis. Or the empty space where Robin had never sat.

"You won't just live in this new world," Teacher said. "You'll lead it."

Nobody uttered a word, or even a gasp. It was too large. Too confusing. The kids at the desert ranch would lead the world? *The whole world?*

Finally, Jay raised his hand. At times like these, Eider felt thankful for him and his stupid questions.

"What do you mean, lead the world?" he asked.

It was the kind of question Teacher usually waved away, but she didn't this time. She began to pace. The classroom wasn't very large, so she could only take a few steps before turning.

"I've been researching for years," she said. "Many years. And I've confirmed that it's a prophecy shared across cultures, in countless ancient texts: that a child will save the world. That a child shall lead. Out of the darkness. Away from the night.

"It's only natural that one of you—the most brilliant, special, and purehearted, the very, very *best*—is fated to be that child."

After a moment, Finch raised his hand.

"Yes, Finch."

"Only one of us?" he asked.

Teacher nodded. "You'll all be important, of course. You *are* important. But only one of you can lead. That's why I've been observing you so closely. Taking notes. Clocking times.

"The leader won't be just the strongest, or the fastest, or the kindest, or the bravest. Not only the smartest, or the quickest, or the most dedicated, or the most agile. No, it will be whoever most represents all of the above. Combined."

The nervous excitement in Eider's stomach began to curdle.

Because she wasn't the *most* anything. Not the smartest, or the quickest, or the most dedicated, or the most agile. Ever since her rattlesnake fever, Eider *least* represented all of the above. Except for today's Extrasensory lesson—but it was only one lesson, and they hadn't even completed it.

"That's why it's important that you excel in all your lessons," Teacher said. "Now, more than ever before. Every single one of you has potential to lead. But only one of you is the natural leader of the world."

Finch raised his hand again. "But who?"

"Like I said, I'm still determining which one it will be."

Finch shook his head. "No, I mean, if the world has ended and nobody's left . . . who will we be leading?"

Eider clasped her hands together under the table. She couldn't believe what Finch was asking. Would Teacher answer? What would she say?

"Each other," Teacher replied.

"That's all?" Finch asked.

The other kids looked bewildered by Finch's interrogation. Of course they did—they didn't know. They hadn't crouched over the radio and heard the blurry word.

The warning in Teacher's eyes didn't make it to her mouth. She opened it, then closed it. She looked out the window, as though she were turning something over in her mind. When she finally turned back toward the kids, her expression was soft—but resolute.

"Each other," she said again. "And all the Other People, too."

There was a collective pause. Then small sounds from everyone, like evening crickets. Uncertainty, confusion. Surprise over what Teacher had said. And from Eider and Finch, surprise that she'd said it at all.

Other People.

Teacher had admitted it. She'd admitted she'd been keeping a secret from them—a colossal one. Even if she hadn't told untruths outright, she'd hidden the truth. Not by mistake, but on purpose.

Linnet lifted one small hand. "So . . . the world didn't end?"

"It did," Teacher said. "It did end—that's a fact."

"Oh."

"Everywhere but here. But that doesn't mean everything has vanished entirely. Anything that remains has changed for the worse. Like the sea. Right, Eider?"

Eider started chewing her thumbnail.

"And that's the problem." At last, Teacher stopped pacing and took her seat at the head of the table. She leaned forward, just a little. "Everything has changed for the worse—and every*one*, too. Everyone who's left. They're not like us here, at the desert ranch. They have ill in their hearts. They're dangerous—even evil."

Eider and Finch glanced at each other. His face mirrored her distress.

"Evil," Teacher said again. "And that's why you're here, at the desert ranch. Staying safe, until you've finished your lessons and training. Until we know which one of you is ready to lead the world."

Eider was startled to feel her own hand rise.

"Yes, Eider?"

"But if anything left is for the worse . . ." she began,

"and any Other People are bad, or evil . . . what's there to save? What's the point?"

"That *is* the point." Teacher thumped her fist on the table. "You're all brilliant and special and good. You have the ability to make it better. To save the world. To help the world begin again. The point is *you*."

Eider's nervousness started to feel like excitement again.

"Will everything good come back?" Linnet asked.

Teacher nodded. Her eyes were bright, like lanterns burned behind them. "Everything," she said, "and more."

At that, Eider couldn't help it. She grinned. Beside her, Finch was grinning too. Which meant everyone else started grinning. Even Teacher.

They were brilliant and special.

They were going to save the world.

"I was always going to tell you, of course," Teacher said. "I was just waiting for the right time. Which wasn't going to be today, but of course it's too late now." She turned to Avis. "Do you understand why Extrasensory is so important, Avis?"

"I think so," Avis replied.

"Good. Because I don't want you making a scene like that ever again. We'll have a little talk after the other kids leave."

Avis glanced at Eider, then back at Teacher. She sank a little lower in her chair. "Okay," she mumbled.

As the rest of the kids headed for the door, Teacher's voice sounded stronger, more powerful than ever. "Never forget," she said. "Some people were put on this earth to live. You were put on this earth to soar."

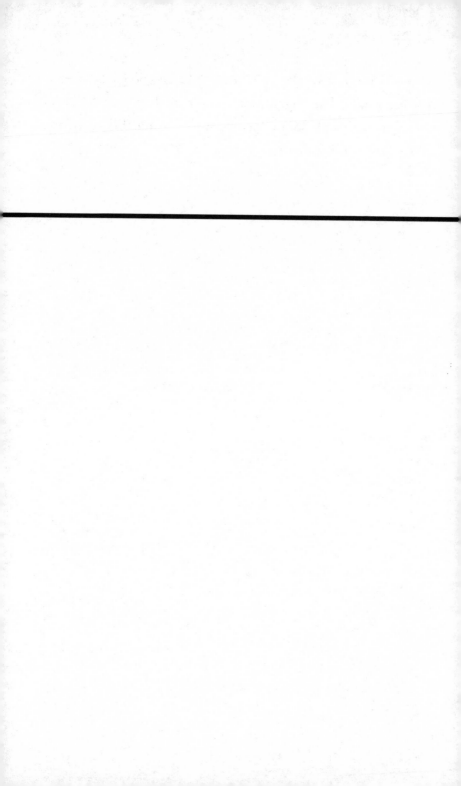

16

ALLIES, NOT ENEMIES

EVERYTHING CHANGED ONCE THE KIDS LEARNED THE TRUTH.

Not in any distinct way. But it was always in the background, like the crackly hum from Finch's radio. A new kind of energy, aimed at each other.

"The world deserves the best," Teacher said. "Strength. Intelligence. Determination. Perseverance. The world's natural leader will be whoever most represents these traits, combined."

Everything came together. The way Eider had imagined the scroll of history, unfurling toward them. All their structure, all their lessons—Physical, Practical, and especially Extrasensory—suddenly made sense.

The kids at the desert ranch were the best and the most brilliant and special. But one of them was better and more brilliant and special than the others. And now they knew Teacher was trying to figure out who.

"You're in competition—but remember, you're not at war. You're allies. Not enemies."

—

Actually, things did change in one distinct way—Avis's braid was gone.

After Avis returned from her talk with Teacher, Eider had wanted to confront her over what had happened at Extrasensory. But at the sight of her, Eider instantly forgot. "What happened?" she exclaimed.

Avis touched her hair. It was chin-length and shaggy. Even a little bit crooked, like she'd just lopped off her long, red braid. "Oh," she said breezily. "I guess it was time to try something different."

"But you love your hair. . . ."

Avis's expression made Eider shut up. They stared at each other in silence, until Eider saw tears in Avis's eyes.

"I can fix it if you want," Eider said, her anger falling away. "If we can get our hands on some scissors."

"Don't worry about it." Avis paused. "Eider, listen. I'm really sorry about—"

"Shh. It's okay." Eider looped her arm through her best friend's.

They were allies, not enemies.

Eider tried to remember that over the next few days,

and the next few days after that. Even though everybody's eyes had gone a little shifty. When Eider lifted hers during a meal, she'd often catch another kid looking at her, then looking away.

Except sometimes Jay didn't look away. He'd keep looking.

More than that, everybody was trying harder. Including Eider. Even when half of their Extrasensory lessons seemed impossible. Like telekinesis: moving objects with their minds. Or levitation: using their minds to lift an object—or each other. While the others giggled, Eider took it seriously.

And Teacher noticed.

FINCH
EIDER
LINNET
AVIS   JAY

Maybe because Eider wasn't just trying harder during her Extrasensory lessons, but during Practical and Physical too. Instead of examining her fairytale book and the papers inside, more often she found herself with her notebook, rereading that day's notes. A couple times, she even sat in the classroom during Free Play and skimmed the earlier World Books.

On purpose!

She found it more interesting than she'd thought she would. Topics that hadn't made much sense when they'd studied A and B and C now had more meaning, and they spread it to the topics around them.

And Physical. Eider had never liked Physical. She liked walking—she could walk forever and ever, she sometimes thought. But all the obstacle courses, the methodical running and jumping and *hop hop hop*, she hated. Compared to the other kids, she wasn't any good.

But was that *because* she didn't like it?

Eider decided to try not hating Physical. She couldn't love it, but she could care. And after a while . . . Well, she still wasn't the best at Physical. That was still Avis and Jay. But Eider beat herself time and again.

One day, Linnet almost caught up to her halfway through a race. Eider pushed through the pinch in her side and ran faster—and faster, and faster, until she rocketed through the finish line just behind Avis.

"Very good, Eider," Teacher said.

Eider hadn't heard that during Physical in a long time, if ever. She glowed.

Until she caught Avis watching her.

Ever since Teacher's little talk, Avis had been acting quieter. More subdued. Not only during Extrasensory—which she hadn't gotten any better at—but during Physical and Practical, too. Almost like her haircut had changed her personality.

Eider didn't really get it. Sure, Avis had loved her braid. But hair grew back, right?

—

An unexpected bonus of being so busy: Eider didn't have time to remember Robin.

For so long, forgetting had been an *action*. Something Eider did on purpose. Actively chasing away her memories-that-weren't, the same way Nurse shooed kit foxes from the garbage pails sometimes. "Get out of here, you rascal," he'd say, waving a wooden spoon.

But now, Eider often went at least half a day without remembering.

Sometimes Eider caught Finch looking at her meaningfully, the way he had before. She knew he wanted to listen to the radio again. Once, she was pretty sure she heard him whisper, "*Eider*," outside her window, but she pretended to be asleep.

Sneaking out just didn't seem worth it.

Last time they'd tried, they'd barely heard anything. Maybe it hadn't even been a voice—just something automatic, like airplanes. Or even wind, maybe. Howling wind. And even if it *had* been actual people—they were dangerous and ill-hearted, like everybody left. They didn't matter. They were pointless.

Eider didn't want to get caught sneaking over something

pointless. Especially now that Teacher had told them the truth. A truth that involved something different. Something *more*.

All Eider had wanted was a point. Now there was one.

EIDER
FINCH
LINNET
JAY
AVIS

17

SECRETS

"**HOW ARE YOU FEELING, KIDDO?**" Nurse asked as Eider sat down for her checkup.

"Good," Eider said. Her usual answer was "Okay," but today it sounded too melancholy for a potential leader.

"That's not as good as great."

"Actually, I feel amazing!"

Nurse chuckled. Eider cooperated as he checked her ears, tonsils, heartbeat, and reflexes. He locked his implements in the cupboard, then leaned back in his chair. The overhead light zinged off his flat, bald head. "I hear you're doing a lot better in your lessons," he said.

Eider perked up even more. "You heard? From who? Did Avis tell you?"

"Teacher told me."

"Wow." Saying "Very good" or "Nice work" to Eider's

face was one thing. Telling Nurse when Eider wasn't around was another.

"I was overjoyed to hear it, kiddo. We've been worried about you for a long time. Ever since the incident."

Eider's smile faded. "I know."

"You've been through a lot, of course. That fever. That horrible snakebite." Nurse shook his head. "Why'd you take off in the first place, anyway? I'm not sure you've ever shared with me."

Eider bit her thumbnail. She liked Nurse—but often, she felt like Teacher was looking out through his eyes. Speaking through his voice.

"Just wanted to see what was out there, I guess." She shrugged. "It was stupid. We didn't realize—"

"We?"

Eider paused, then realized her mistake. "Me, I meant! Only me. I don't think about—anymore. Not at all."

Nurse looked like he didn't quite believe her. But it wasn't a disappointed look. More than anything, it seemed a little sad. "Teacher is always right, of course. It really is for the best. But I'm sure it feels like a big loss, all the same."

Agreeing felt risky, so Eider just shrugged.

"Teacher understands loss, you know," Nurse went on. "For some people, the world didn't end just once. In fact, you could say we've all lost something. Or someone."

She felt unsure what he was getting at. "Teacher lost someone?"

Nurse turned and began to organize his jar of tongue depressors. Even though it was already organized. "Oh, that was a very long time ago."

"But what do you mean, the world didn't end just once?"

"You're all done, kiddo," Nurse said in a singsong voice. "I'll see you at dinner. I have this idea for pickle rice. Sure, it doesn't sound too enticing when I say it, but I think it'll be awfully *delicious*. . . ."

Eider sighed. She wasn't little anymore, and she found Nurse's childlike distractions maddening. "Isn't it better that I know? Especially if the world's going to begin again?"

Nurse blinked at her, like her question had startled him. "You kids are getting smarter and smarter. Where has the time gone?" He shook his head and sighed. "Well, they say the desert's good for old bones, anyway."

"Who does?" Eider asked.

"Oh, nobody. All that matters is what Teacher says."

"Do *you* always do what Teacher says?"

"Of course." Nurse raised an eyebrow. "Do you?"

—

As the kids waited for Teacher to arrive for Circle Time, they sat farther apart than they used to. Staring at their hands and feet instead of each other.

Eider, too. She still didn't know what Nurse had meant about the world ending more than once, but it had left her feeling unsettled. She couldn't help biting her thumbnail as Teacher sat in front of them.

"Good afternoon," she said.

The kids never knew what to expect during Circle Time. Funny stories, or serious discussion. Teacher's expression usually predicted the tone of her talks. Right now, she looked serious.

Very, very serious.

"Today, we're going to talk about honesty," Teacher said. "It's one of the most important qualities in a leader. I'm going to ask a question, and I expect an honest answer. Do you understand?"

The kids all nodded.

"Who took my permanent marker?"

Now the all kids glanced at each other, brows furrowed.

"I left it on the table during Practical. When I returned, it was missing. Markers are very valuable—it's not like I can go to the store and purchase one. Who took it?"

Eider scanned the circle again. Everybody looked confused. Only Linnet's expression was different: her bottom lip trembling, like she might cry. Because Eider couldn't tell her to knock it off, she raised her hand.

"Maybe . . . you dropped it somewhere?" she asked.

Teacher's glare was cactus-sharp. "That isn't possible. Somebody here is keeping a secret. I'm certain. And it's made me wonder what else you've been hiding."

Eider had an urge to chew her thumbnails, so she sat on her hands.

"We can't read each other's minds," Teacher went on, "no matter how much Extrasensory we practice. Not entirely. That's why honesty is so important."

She leaned forward, just a bit.

"Having secrets is part of being human. But every single child in this room is more than human. You're *super*-human."

"Superhuman?" Jay repeated.

"That's right," Teacher said firmly. "Which is why I expect much, much more of you. Total honesty. Total trustworthiness. Secrets benefit nobody but the person they belong to. I want no more secrets—starting right now.

"Are any of you keeping a secret?"

Everybody froze. Bracing themselves for each other to speak. Every single one of them had secrets.

But Eider had the most.

The gap in the fence. The stuff she'd found for Finch. The shard she'd given Linnet. The fairytale book—packed with windborne papers, Eider's biggest secret of all. Or maybe the radio was the biggest secret? Technically, that secret belonged to Finch. But Eider wasn't sure that would matter to Teacher.

"How about someone else's secret?" Teacher asked, her eyes candle-bright. "Keeping secrets for others is just as dangerous. Share now . . . and I won't be angry."

Still, silence. The tension in the room grew thicker and thicker.

Eider couldn't look at Finch, so she glanced at Avis—who

was staring at her hands. Avis knew so many of Eider's secrets. But she'd never tell on Eider. Right?

Finally, Teacher sighed. "I'll give you a little longer. Remember, if you share any secrets you know about first, I'll be more understanding when you share your own. And of course, if any more supplies go missing . . . I just might decide studying is more important than Free Play. You're dismissed."

As they walked away, Eider kept her head down, same as everyone else. She couldn't stop thinking about her fairy-tale book.

After she'd learned Robin was imaginary, she'd felt so lonely. That was why she'd wanted to share the book. For some reason, she'd chosen Avis—the right choice, she knew now, because they'd been best friends ever since. Though Avis wasn't particularly interested in reading stories, she'd seemed to treasure the secret; to take its keeping seriously. She had for years.

Even if Avis didn't tell on her, could Eider be sure she'd hidden the book exactly right? What would happen if Teacher found it? And *opened* it? Saw all the scraps of paper Eider had collected and stuck inside?

The secret-keeping alone was bad enough. But even more than that, it was what those scraps of paper repre-sented. Looking backward instead of forward. Outward instead of inward. What Teacher always suspected Eider was guilty of doing.

She'd take away Eider's book, like she had all the other books. Maybe she'd even destroy it.

Eider had wanted a point and now she had one. A reason to care about lessons, even obstacle courses. A deeper meaning for their existence at the desert ranch, after the end of the world, so far from Beyond and Before.

The fairytale book was the opposite of all that.

It broke Eider's heart . . .

But she had to get rid of it before Teacher did.

18

INTREPID EXPLORER

As Eider approached the storage room during Free Play, she was half-afraid she'd find the door wide open, the fairytale book magically unearthed. Its pages glowing brightly.

But Eider found it under the floorboard, just where she'd left it. Dusty, but that wasn't unusual. The desert always found its way inside.

She picked it up, relieved. Her fingers lingered over Cinderella and her pumpkin coach. Eider couldn't remember the last time she'd opened the book—a few weeks ago, at least. Not since she'd stashed the housing-development pamphlet inside.

She had an urge to flip through it one last time.

She couldn't bear to.

How to hide it? She considered wrapping the book in her jacket, but that would look almost as suspicious as carrying it openly. Finally, she stuffed it down the front of her overalls. The corners stuck out, but it was better than nothing.

Outside, Eider paused to make sure the coast was clear. Then she hurried up the rise, the fastest path to the date grove. She'd only made it halfway when the book slipped out the side of her overalls.

She tried not to yelp as it went *bump-bump-bump* down the slope, landing in a patch of creosote. The postcard had come loose—the rectangle paper with the desert-flower drink.

Dear Roland,
Bet you could use one of these right now! Wish you were here.
Love,
Mandy

She recovered the book, shoving the postcard back inside.

"Hey, Eider!"

Eider whirled around. It was Linnet, her hands in her overalls pockets, a shy smile on her face. Her notebook was tucked under one arm.

"Where are you going?" she asked.

"Just for a walk," Eider said.

"Can I come?"

"No! Sorry, I—I'd like to be alone. Maybe next time."

But Linnet didn't take the hint. "Is that a book?"

Eider stuffed the fairytale book inside her overalls. "Is that your notebook?" she shot back. "I hope you're not still secretly drawing in it. It's not worth it, you know."

Linnet took a step backward. "I know," she said softly.

"Look, I've got to go."

Eider turned and jogged toward the fence, already feeling a little regretful. But right now, she needed fewer secrets, not more of them.

———

Eider squeezed though the gap in the fence, careful not to snag her overalls. She headed for the ravine, the direction she usually went.

Then she stopped.

She needed a better hiding spot than her same old places. If she buried the fairytale book just a few feet from the desert ranch—well, she doubted anybody would find it. Possibly Finch, if he ever snuck out again, but it wasn't the kind of thing he'd find useful, anyway. She wasn't worried about that.

She was worried about herself.

If the book was too close, it'd be too easy to retrieve.

Eider started walking again. Not alongside the fence, but perpendicular to it. Away from the desert ranch.

Although the route was brand-new, her boots knew exactly which kinds of earth to step on and which kinds to avoid. She'd forgotten how exhilarating it felt, walking out here in the desert silence. Why did it seem like so long ago?

Because Eider hadn't even been *thinking* about exploring.

Ever since Teacher's talk about leaders, Eider hadn't thought about exploring, or the sea, or her fairytale book, or the housing-development pamphlet she'd tucked inside. She hadn't been thinking of Finch's radio, or the grainy voice it had captured. She'd been thinking of her lessons. The way Teacher had always wanted her to.

And it had felt *good*. Doing what Teacher said. Earning her approval, at long last.

But not as good as exploring. Every time Eider stepped outside the fence, her thoughts did too. She could think about Beyond and Before without feeling guilty or wrong. She could think about Robin.

"I'm burying the book," Eider said out loud, making it real.

She walked down a slope. Up a rise and down another. When she glanced over her shoulder, she couldn't see the spike at all. It was lost in a pleat of hills. Which meant this was farther out than she'd ever been.

Other than that one time, with Robin.

Eider closed her eyes. No matter how strong she thought she was, her sister always found her way in. Memories-that-weren't, tapping into dreams and daylight. Shutting off that part of her brain had been a relief, even if only for a while.

But out here, Eider felt a sharp pang of *missing*. Almost like she'd lost her sister all over again.

"The book," Eider said again.

Kneeling, she set the book under a shrub and began to dig.

"Hey!"

It was a small, faraway voice. But it hadn't come from the desert ranch, lost in the hills behind her. It had come from someplace in front of her.

And then Eider saw him. A person—a grown-up person. Not Teacher or Nurse or the Handyman, but somebody Eider didn't recognize.

Other People.

"Hey you!" the man called.

Eider's heart began to pound. She couldn't move. She just stood there as the man approached, heading closer, heading for *her*.

His face was nut-brown and scruffy, like he hadn't shaved in weeks. He wore a dirty red bandana around his forehead. His shoes were dingy, lumpy things with ridged soles, and his backpack was almost as big as he was.

Eider had longed to see Other People her whole life. But now that one of them was standing in front of her, all she could think of were Teacher's words:

They're dangerous. Even evil.

"Are you on a hike, too?" the man asked.

Eider glanced over her shoulder, but it was too late to run. The man would be faster, anyway. Maybe Jay or Avis could beat him, but definitely not Eider.

"No habla inglés?" the man tried.

"Huh?"

"Oh—I just thought you might not speak English. What are you doing here?"

"I—" Eider swallowed twice, but she couldn't dislodge the knot of fear in her throat. "I live here."

The man's eyes grew wide. "You're telling me you live way out here?"

She nodded.

"Wow, we must be—how many miles?" He shrugged, then shook his head. "What a life that must be. Are you bussed into school, or . . . ?"

Eider wasn't sure what he meant. "I go to school here."

"Ah, so you're homeschooled. That makes sense." The man pulled off his red bandana and wiped his face with it, but it only smeared the dirt around. "Still. Even a few hours hiking out here've got me broiled like a steak. You must be a tough, tough kid."

She shrugged.

"I mean it. I have a daughter back home—a daughter and a son, actually. Both older than you. But they hate the desert. 'It's too dirty,' my son says. My daughter would rather lounge around and play video games." He smiled. "Pretty annoying, right?"

Eider's head swam. Back home? A daughter and a son? She didn't even know what video games were. But she liked the way the man smiled when he talked about his kids. Like he wasn't *really* annoyed by them.

"Do you go exploring a lot?" he asked.

"I . . . used to. Not as much anymore."

"But you're familiar with this area?"

She shrugged again. "Only sort of."

"Well, maybe you can help me anyway. I heard there was an abandoned military outpost around these parts. Do you know what I'm talking about? Have you seen it?"

A military outpost? Again, Eider wasn't sure what he meant. She shook her head. "I don't think so."

"Hold on." The man pulled out a rectangular device from his pocket, tapped it a few times, then held it out to her. "See, it looks like this."

Eider didn't want to go any closer, but curiosity won out.

She took a couple steps and peered at the man's device. There were pictures on it, like her glossy rectangles— except these pictures *glowed*. Even in the sunlight. And when the man touched them with his finger, they moved! Eider's papers didn't do that. She knew magic didn't exist, but Finch's ones and zeroes couldn't explain it either. Right?

She wished Finch was here. Or Avis. Or even Linnet. At the very least, they'd be able to confirm that Eider wasn't having another fever dream.

"Camp Douglas, it used to be called," the man said. He tapped his device again, and a map appeared. "Closed back in the fifties. Most of it's gone, but there are supposed to be these great big concrete slabs left. Sound familiar?"

Concrete slabs?

"Oh!" Eider exclaimed. "They're—"

She stopped.

Somehow, she'd momentarily forgotten Teacher's warnings about Other People. About the danger and the evil. How could it have slipped her mind? Because the man was so friendly. And funny. Because he had a *family*.

But that didn't guarantee anything, did it?

"Maybe over that way?" Eider said, pointing the wrong direction.

"Are you sure?"

She nodded. "There's three of them. About fifteen feet by fifteen feet."

"That's exactly right." The man glanced at his magic device again and put it back into his pocket. "Well, sometimes these things go all wonky way out here. Not enough towers." He knelt to tighten the laces on one of his huge, lumpy shoes.

"Your shoes are so big," Eider blurted.

He nodded and smiled. "I know they don't look like much, but underneath the grime they're state-of-the-art. Good shoes are every journey's most important companion. I'd never make it a hundred feet without 'em."

Eider glanced down at her own boots. They were just as grimy, now that she was looking at them. She wished she had better shoes. At least she wasn't wearing ballet slippers. She coughed, trying to clear the sudden ache in her throat.

"Thanks for the help, intrepid explorer," the man said. "What's your name?"

"Eider," she told him.

"Eider. That's interesting. Like eiderdown?"

She stared at him blankly.

"Eiderdown. The feathers in pillows. They come from the eider bird. It's a duck-like thing, I think . . . no?" He shrugged. "Anyway, nice to meet you. I'm Charles. Charles the Hiker."

"Nice to meet you, Charles the Hiker."

He put out his dirty hand, and Eider shook it.

She watched him hike away, his lumpy blue shoes crunching the desert sameness, until he disappeared into the hills.

She waited a little longer.

Then she ran toward the fence without looking back.

—

Eider hid in the date grove for the rest of Free Play, crouching among the trees. She kept quiet all through dinner (black beans and boiled potatoes—probably yuck, but Eider didn't eat any), watching the other kids practice their telepathy skills. Which meant nothing was happening.

"What're you looking at, cloudface?" Jay asked.

"I'm practicing telepathy, too," Eider said. "Ew, Jay. You're gross. Why are you thinking about that?"

Jay's eyes widened. "I wasn't—whatever. Go away."

After dinner, Linnet called Eider's name. "Could I talk to you?" she asked.

Eider shook her head. "Not right now."

"But—"

"I said I can't talk right now, Linnet!"

Eider jogged straight for her trailer, hoping Linnet wouldn't follow. It wasn't time for bed yet, but she climbed onto her bed and scooted against the wall, hugging her knees, as the sky outside the window deepened into blue evening. At some point she heard the other girls come in, but she pretended to be asleep.

Eider didn't know what to do. Or even what to think. Her thoughts spun around and around in her head, all except one:

Am I really named after a pillow?

She felt like a pillow. Soft and useless. Push too hard and she'd explode into fluff: windborne, air and nothing.

Eider had met someone from Beyond. An *Other Person*, with lumpy shoes and moving-picture magic. Not dangerous-seeming in the slightest. Or suffering. He seemed like he was doing just fine. He was cheerful, even!

And all Eider had done was stand there, gaping like a dead sea fish. Then she'd sent him the wrong way. She hoped he'd made it home okay. Wherever home was. In a desert ranch, like theirs? Or in a town? A city?

Where did Other People live?

Eider was desperate to know more. But it might be *years* before Teacher told them. Who could Eider ask, besides Teacher? Nurse was useless. The Handyman wouldn't even talk to the kids. And besides them, no voices entered the desert ranch but Teacher's.

Then again . . .

Eider sat up in bed.

A DISEASE OF
THE MIND

EIDER HAD NEVER ENTERED THE BOYS' TRAILER AT NIGHT. But there was a first time for everything.

Jay was snoring with his mouth open. No wonder Finch hadn't heard her tapping. Eider poked Finch in the side until he woke.

"Ow!" Finch protested. "Why're you girls always poking me?"

"Sorry. Can you come outside? I need to talk to you, but I don't want to wake Jay."

"Jay sleeps like a boulder." Grudgingly, Finch pulled on his boots and followed Eider down the steps.

"So I've been thinking about your radio . . ." Eider began.

Finch looked like he'd been struck.

"Why do you look so— Finch, I'd never tell Teacher on

you! Don't you know that?" The relief in his face annoyed her. "That's not what this is about. It's just been so long since we've listened to your radio, and I've been thinking about it. About the voice we heard."

"Just one word," he said. "Nothing ever again."

"But we never tried again."

Finch raised his eyebrows, until it dawned on Eider that of course he'd tried again. On his own. It bothered Eider, even though it was her own fault for ignoring his meaningful glances. Now she understood why Avis hated being left out.

"Okay, fine," she said. "But . . . wouldn't we only hear it when somebody is broadcasting? So like, at certain times? Or certain days of the week?"

"Maybe, but how would we know? We can't just leave it on constantly."

"Well, sure. But what I'm saying is—I don't think we've given it enough of a chance. I think we need to try more. We know Other People are out there. Teacher confirmed it!"

"Evil people."

"But do you really think *everyone* is evil?"

Finch lifted one shoulder.

"Because I don't. Because . . ." Eider lowered her voice to the slightest breath of air, softer than a whisper. "I met somebody when I was exploring. A man."

Finch froze. Long enough that she wondered if he

hadn't understood her. But he had. "I'll meet you at the slabs in ten minutes."

—

Eider told Finch all about Charles the Hiker.

She'd been hesitant at first. Secrets were a bigger deal than ever now. If Teacher somehow got it out of Finch that Eider had met a real, live Other Person out there in the desert and hadn't run to tell her . . .

Discipline seemed like a bigger deal now, too.

More possible, anyway. But Eider trusted Finch—lately, more than anyone. And so, she described the hiker's beard, his red bandana, his lumpy blue shoes. Her description of the moving-picture device set a fire in his eyes. But not as much as her insistence that Charles hadn't seemed evil, or dangerous, or even ill-hearted—that he'd been *nice*.

"And funny," Eider said.

At that, Finch laughed. Eider did too. How funny that the man had been funny.

For the next few days, they listened to the radio every night. It didn't seem to matter where they met: at the slabs, in the storage room, underneath the date palms. All they heard was the dull, grainy roar.

In the daytime, they continued with their lessons, as usual: *hop-hop-hopping* through obstacle course tires, tackling increasingly harder Extrasensory lessons, jotting down notes from the World Book. In Practical, the kids finished R and moved on to S, which was two whole volumes long: S–Sn, and So–Sz.

One afternoon during Free Play, Eider thumbed through the first volume. The pages for Sea were missing. It didn't really matter—they'd studied Ocean ages ago. But it was strange, just the same. The way Radio had been missing, too.

Was it a coincidence? Or did it have deeper meaning?

It was hard to tell.

During Quiet Time one evening, Finch was late to the date grove. Eider waited in the trees, listening to the breeze shudder the palm fronds. She marveled at how dark it was without her penlight on. Dark, though nowhere near complete.

She thought about her fairytale book. She had no idea where she'd left it—just sitting someplace, under a shrub. Her heart ached, remembering. It'd get ruined for sure. The desert devoured anything left outside for long.

At least she'd memorized everything inside. Well, everything except the housing-development pamphlet, though she could still picture the dark-haired family when she closed her eyes.

A footstep crunched nearby. Eider hid behind a palm trunk until she was sure it was Finch.

"Sorry I'm late," he said. "Jay wanted to talk."

"About what?"

"Avis. He says he has a crush on her."

"Really?" Eider's mouth fell open. "Jay and Avis? They hate each other!"

"I guess not."

"Finch, don't you think maybe that's the sort of thing you should have kept to yourself?"

Finch blinked, then blinked again. "Oh. I don't know. I hadn't thought about it."

"It's kind of obvious!" Eider couldn't suppress a giggle. "Sometimes you seem like a man from the moon. Anyway. Did anyone see you come out here?"

"Teacher is in her office. Jay's asleep."

"Great." Eider sat down with her back against a palm, watching Finch set up the radio. It still resembled a broken robot. She wondered what it would have looked like if the Radio section hadn't been missing. "Hey, Finch?"

"Yeah?"

"Why do you think pages are missing from the World Books?"

He glanced at her. "I'm not sure. They're super old—could be lots of reasons."

"You don't think there's anything . . ." Eider tried to choose her words carefully. ". . . anything *on purpose* about it? Like, about the particular pages that are missing?"

"What do you mean?"

She shrugged, because she wasn't sure herself. Only half-formed thoughts going *tap-tap-tap* on her brain. "I guess I'm just wondering if they have something in common."

"Hmm," Finch said. His fingers began their usual

dance, jostling wires, tapping knobs, and so forth. And suddenly, the grainy hum became a voice.

"Don't move!" Eider whispered.

. . . *STORM.*

"Okay, that was definitely *storm*," Finch said.

IT'S IMPORTANT THAT . . .
WHEN . . . THE STORM COMING . . .

"Is this one of your news reports?" Eider asked.
"How would I know?" Finch said. "Shh."

AS LONG AS WE . . .
. . . IS A THREAT.
. . . THE SPECIAL ONES. WHEN THE DANGER ARRIVES . . .
UNLESS . . . NOBODY WILL BE SAFE.

A half minute passed, where they couldn't make out anything. Then:

. . . BECAUSE THE END IS VERY NEAR.

Then a click, and the raspy, blurry voice vanished into silence. No grainy roar or dusty hum. Nothing.

"Wow," Eider said, the only word she could manage.

"Yeah," Finch agreed.

They sat there a moment longer. Then he shut off the radio.

—

Eider had just climbed into bed when the alarm began.

Eeeeeee. Eeeeeee. Eeeeeee.

Her stomach dropped. What if it had sounded a few minutes earlier, when they'd been at the slabs? She didn't know which worried her more, now: the threat of discipline, or the potential danger.

WHEN THE DANGER ARRIVES . . .

"Hurry!" shouted Avis, pulling on her boots.

The boys were already in the shelter when the girls arrived. Jay, looking groggy. And Finch, looking panicked— because he was holding the radio.

"Finch!" Eider said with a gasp. "I can't believe you brought that!"

"I didn't have enough time to hide it. . . ."

"Hide what?" Avis asked.

"Yeah, what is that, anyway?" Jay asked, a little less groggy now.

Finch hid the radio behind his back. "Just a contraption."

"A *what?* Let me see."

Jay made a grab for it, but Eider knocked his arm away. "It's none of your business!" she shouted, planting herself in front of him. Linnet backed into a corner, sniffling.

"So it's a secret?" Jay said. "What would Teacher think about it?"

"Is that supposed to be a threat, you oaf? I didn't tell anyone about your creepy collection!"

"Don't call it creepy! You know it isn't!"

"What's he talking about?" Avis asked Eider.

"Not now, Avis. Jay, this is important—"

"Then when?" Avis interrupted. "What else aren't you telling me, Eider?"

"Nothing! I—"

The shelter door opened, and they all went quiet. They must have missed the sound of the key in the lock. "I heard yelling," Nurse said. "What's going on?"

"Nothing," all five kids said at once.

Nurse rarely noticed anything. But he noticed Finch's arms behind his back, the nervous-rabbit twitch in his face. "What's that you've got there, buddy?"

"It's nothing."

"It doesn't look like nothing. Give it here."

With shaking hands, Finch surrendered his radio.

Nurse's brow furrowed as he examined it. "Is this a . . . ? No, it can't be. But then again . . ." He ran a hand over his flat, bald head. "I think Teacher needs to know about this. Come along with me, Finch."

Finch stumbled after Nurse, head hanging. Eider followed. So did the other kids. If Nurse saw, he didn't stop them.

He knocked on the door to Teacher's office. She opened it, then, seeing everyone, slipped out too quickly for Eider to peek inside.

"What is it?" Teacher asked Nurse irritably. "Why'd you— What are they all doing here? There was an alarm. What are you thinking?"

"I know, but—" Nurse began.

"All I ask is that you do as I say. It could be dangerous."

Nurse's cheeks were pink now. "Of course, of course. But I heard them shouting. When I opened the door, Finch was holding this." He handed over the radio.

Teacher examined it, turning it over. She wasn't gentle with it, like Finch was. "Is this a *radio*? Finch, where did you get this?"

"I—I made it," he replied.

"How could you possibly? Where did you get the parts?"

"Um . . ." He swallowed. "Here and there, you know. Around."

"I'm sure," Teacher said, in a voice that clearly meant the opposite. "Is it functional? Did you hear anything?"

"I—"

"All we heard was crackling," Eider interjected.

Teacher's eyes blazed in her direction. "You were part of this, too?"

"She didn't build it," Finch said. "That was only me."

"Yeah," Eider said, "but I encouraged him. I helped him look for the parts."

"No, she didn't, I did that all on my own—"

"Quiet!" Teacher held up a hand. "I know you both. Better even than you know yourselves. Eider couldn't build something like this without Finch's help. And Finch wouldn't build something like this without Eider's encouragement."

Eider and Finch looked at each other. "That's not . . ." they began in unison, then stopped.

"It doesn't even work," Avis said.

"So you knew about this, too?" Teacher said.

Avis turned violet. "I don't . . . I didn't . . ."

In one swift motion, Teacher slammed the radio onto the ground.

Crunch.

Now it really did look like a broken robot. Finch jerked toward it, but Eider grabbed his elbow to stop him. Even Nurse looked shocked.

"You're very smart, Finch." The calm in Teacher's voice was more frightening than any shout. "I should have known that one of these days, your curiosity might steer you in the wrong direction. It's a strong force—a disease, almost. A disease of the mind."

"But I—" Finch began, but Teacher held up a hand again.

"Should I take the kiddos back to the shelter?" Nurse asked.

Teacher glared at him. "It was just a drill," she said. "Finch, I'd like you to meet me in the classroom before breakfast tomorrow. It's time for a little talk."

———

Eider worried late into the night. About the radio broadcast and its confusing, chilling words. About Finch and what his discipline might be.

Even when she managed to fall asleep, the apprehension swirled into her dreams. She was trapped alone while the world raged outside: storms, tidal waves, the *zap-bang-pow* of a war that wasn't games at all.

Bang. Bang. Bang.

Those weren't dream sounds—they were real. Eider sat up in bed. The faintest light shone through the trailer windows. It was morning, but barely.

Bang. Bang. Bang.

"What is that?" she asked.

"I'll bet it's the Handyman," Avis replied from her bed.

"Are you sure?" Linnet asked.

"If it was a danger, there'd be an alarm, wouldn't there? Go back to sleep."

But Eider couldn't sleep, not until she knew for sure. Even though it was risky, she pulled on her boots and slipped outside, then jogged to the top of the rise.

Avis had been right. From Eider's vantage point, she could see the Handyman crouched beside the fence—right where the gap was. Tall wooden planks were stacked on the ground beside him.

As she watched, he took a piece of wood and leaned it against another.

Bang. Bang. Bang.

20

THE SPACE BETWEEN

FINCH WASN'T AT BREAKFAST THE NEXT DAY. At lunch, he arrived at the dining area late and ate his meal (spotted beans and brown rice, just okay) without looking up.

Had he gotten disciplined?

Eider couldn't tell. His eyes looked a little puffy, but otherwise, he seemed normal. She was still dying to discuss what they'd heard on the radio, but she needed to know he was okay first.

As they passed under the twin windmills after lunch, she managed to grab his arm.

"I'm so sorry, Finch," she whispered.

He shook her off. "It's okay. Forget it."

"But it was my fault, as much as it was yours. Did you get disciplined?"

Finch nodded. The windmills spun overhead, his face

changing from sun to shade, sun to shade. "She took my . . ." He cringed, as if the agony was too great to bear. "She took my notebooks."

"Your notebooks?" Eider had braced herself for something truly terrible. Now a snort of laughter escaped. "That's all? That's not bad."

"Maybe not for *you*."

"But they were only World Book notes, right? Who cares! You can always read the books again—"

"It wasn't just World Book notes."

Eider paused. "Oh."

"I had lots in there. Plans, and ideas, and—and other things. She knew. She knew what I cared the most about, and she took it away."

Avis's haircut, Eider realized. It had happened after her little talk with Teacher. Something twisted deep in Eider's middle. "Can we get them back?"

"No, she—she burned them." Finch looked like he was trying not to cry. "Now what's the point? What's the point of doing anything anymore?"

"Finch, you can't think that way. . . ."

"How would you feel, Eider? If you lost the thing that mattered most to you in the entire world?"

Without waiting for her to answer, Finch hurried off.

Eider lingered under the windmills, letting the distance between them grow. Trying not to cry herself. She hated herself for laughing at Finch. For not understanding, even for a moment. Because she realized she *had* been disciplined. And she'd never gotten over it.

How would you feel, Eider? If you lost the thing that mattered most to you in the entire world?

"I did," Eider said softly.

—

In the days that followed, Eider thought things might change again. But in a hopeful way. That after Teacher had destroyed Finch's radio, the kids might come together. Talk openly in ways they never had, about their fears, worries, and doubts.

Instead, the opposite happened—they hardly spoke at all.

The kids at the desert ranch had been more than family. They'd been allies, but also competitors. Now, they acted almost like strangers.

Because Teacher was always watching.

With her clipboard and stopwatch, writing down notes, clocking times. Measuring the kids against one another. Pinning their names against the wall, like the bugs on Jay's board. Waiting to see who'd disobey her.

Deciding what she'd take away next.

Robin not being real was a relief, sometimes. Eider didn't have to worry about losing her. She didn't have to wonder if Robin had made it. What would have happened if she hadn't. If somewhere on her journey west, she'd given up.

The way Eider wanted to.

Eider would never be a leader. She knew it—and Teacher did, too. So what was the point of doing anything anymore?

The radio was broken. Eider had lost her fairytale book and her secret papers. The other kids would barely look at her. She couldn't even explore—the Handyman had closed the gap. Teacher had taken everything away. There was no place left to look but inward.

Just like Teacher had always wanted.

—

After dinner one night, Eider took the long way back to her trailer.

Overhead, the clouds were more spectacular than usual, edged in the ruddy light of sunset. Eider stopped to watch them. She only meant to pause for a moment, but she found she didn't want to look away. Clouds were another type of Beyond, weren't they? So close, and so far, all at the same time.

For the first time in a long while, Eider felt at peace.

She lifted both of her arms, opening her palms to the sky. The light edged her fingers, too. Almost as if the clouds, so many miles away, were touching her.

The space between them doesn't matter as long as they exist.

She curled her hands into fists, taking the red light with them. And then, with her arms held out, she spun.

When she stopped, she saw Linnet watching her.

Eider shrugged and smiled sheepishly. She knew she'd probably looked ridiculous, but at least Linnet wasn't the type to tease. Jay probably would have called her cloudface for the rest of her life.

"Were you dancing?" Linnet asked.

"Dancing?" Eider thought about it. "I guess I was, a little bit."

"I haven't seen you dance in a long time."

Linnet's voice was even more timid than usual. Eider remembered how sharp she'd been with her lately, and felt bad all over again. "Yeah," Eider agreed quietly. "It has been a long time."

"Why?"

"Oh . . ." Eider began, then stopped as tears stung her eyes. She wiped them with the back of her hand. "Oh, I don't know. No reason."

Linnet kept staring at her, the strangest expression on her small face. Eider was the first to look away.

"Linnet, do you remember what I said before? About drawing not being worth it?"

"Yes," she replied.

"Well, I was wrong," Eider said. "Don't stop drawing. Ever."

———

Later that night, the coyotes were overly excitable. Howling, barking, yip-yip-yipping. Eider lay in bed with her fists under her chin, eyes closed, listening to the cacophony. Trying to pick apart separate sounds. She was getting better at it—at least one Extrasensory lesson had stuck.

Although when she thought about it, dance was also a kind of Extrasensory, wasn't it? Somebody wrote the music. Somebody sang it and made the beats. Somebody sent it out, and Teacher's radio captured it. And at the other end of all that space and time, Eider used it to move her body. The music in her head.

"Eider?" As soft as a sigh.

When Eider opened her eyes, she saw Linnet standing over her bed. "What?" she whispered.

Shoulders hunched, Linnet glanced toward Avis, still sleeping. The younger girl really was like a baby mouse, Eider thought. Always frozen before the retreat. Trying her best not to act impatient, Eider patted the edge of her bed.

Gingerly, Linnet sat. "I have something of yours."

"Oh?"

"Well, I'm pretty sure it's yours—I mean, I saw you drop it. . . ." In a flourish, Linnet whipped around her hand and shoved a paper at Eider.

Not just any paper—the housing-development pamphlet. Eider grabbed it and stuffed it under her pillow. *"When?"*

"A while ago," Linnet said. "You were about to go on a walk, and you dropped your—you dropped something. I wanted to give it to you, but you're always so busy. . . ."

"It's okay." Even the feel of the pamphlet made her heart beat faster. "Thank you. For not telling—" She paused. "You didn't tell, right?"

"Of course I didn't!"

Eider smiled a tiny bit. "Did you look at it?"

Linnet was silent.

"It's really okay."

"Yes," Linnet whispered. "It's families."

"Yes," Eider agreed.

"One of them . . . they look like you."

"I thought so, too."

"Like you and Robin."

Everything in Eider went still. "What?"

Linnet glanced at Avis again, still sleeping, then back at Eider. "Robin," Linnet whispered. "I remember her."

"You—you do?" Eider's heart felt too big for her chest.

Linnet nodded. "I—"

Avis rolled over in bed. Linnet jumped to her feet and hurried into her own. A baby mouse, so easily scared. But maybe a little bit brave, too.

Eider rolled over too, hugging her pillow. Her fingers gripped the pamphlet so tightly she knew she was bending it, but she didn't care. She felt like crying. She felt like screaming. She felt like laughing—or like screaming with laughter until she burst into tears. Because now Eider knew. Now she knew for sure.

Robin was real.

21

ONCE UPON A TIME

THE PROBLEM WITH NOBODY TELLING YOU how big the world is—
or *was*—is that you'd never guess it yourself.

How big it is. Not only big: *huge.*

A map means nothing when you can measure a continent in inches.

A mile means little if you're not sure you've walked one.

They thought they could. Walk not only a mile, but many. They thought they could walk anywhere in the entire world on their own two feet. That everything they'd read about and heard about and imagined, even, was just past the horizon.

They thought.

—

Once upon a time, life was good. Teacher didn't even have to remind them.

But that was before Robin's big tantrum.

She'd always been stubborn. But ever since turning six, she acted out more and more. If she didn't want to do something, she'd refuse, or demand to know why. She'd stamp her feet. She'd cry—sometimes on purpose.

Crocodile tears, Teacher called them. "They're make-believe. I don't want to have to discipline you."

A clear threat, but easy to ignore. Discipline didn't seem real back then.

Neither did running away, though Eider and Robin talked about it time and again. Lying on their backs at the slabs, watching the night sky. Talking about families. Wondering when Beyond began—past the horizon, or right at the fence? It was fun to speculate about running away, but never an actual option.

Until it was the only one.

Like most of Robin's tantrums, its spark was minor: something less than delicious at dinnertime. But this kicking, screaming explosion was in front of everyone. Not only Eider and the other kids, but also Teacher and the Handyman and Nurse, who just stood there wringing his hands.

"I can cook something else," he said.

"No," Teacher said. "Robin will finish her meal. She's lucky to eat what she gets."

"I don't have to do anything," Robin shrieked. "You're not my mother. You're not my family."

Teacher grabbed her arm and hauled her to her feet. "That's enough! Go to your trailer. We'll figure out your discipline tomorrow."

That was all it took. Secretly, Eider and Robin gathered their things. They didn't have packs; only cloth bags with handles, worn thin. Eider had hoped the bags would last. It depended on how long the horizon took to reach, and what they'd find on the other side.

At dawn's first gray light, they left.

Since the desert ranch was a planet in a universe of empty space, they could go any direction at all. Robin thought they should head east, toward the early-morning sun. Eider pointed out that before long, it'd pass right over them, and then they'd be walking away from it.

So they headed west.

They'd only walked a few minutes when Robin stopped. "My boot's busted."

"You're kidding." Eider knelt down and checked. Sure enough, the sole was coming away from the rest of the boot. "Why didn't you say anything?"

"I didn't *know*."

Robin was only six. But because she was so smart, Eider often forgot she was the younger sister. That she still needed to be taken care of sometimes.

Eider didn't have any way to fix Robin's boot. To the

east, she could still see the desert ranch. The low point in the fence, which they'd stepped right over. The spike, poking into the hazy morning sky. They could run back home and try to fix it quickly. Or they could set out a different day.

But they'd already come this far—even if it wasn't very far at all. The hardest part was the first step, and Eider didn't want to retrace it. Especially since, at some point soon, Teacher would realize they were missing.

Eider sighed, reached into her bag, and pulled out her ballet slippers. Bringing them had been silly, but she hadn't been able to bear leaving them.

Robin's whole face lit up. "Really? You're gonna let me wear them?"

"It's our best option," Eider said. "They'll be too big, but they're better than nothing. We won't get very far with you barefoot."

She tied them onto Robin's feet the best she could.

"Can you walk?" she asked.

Robin took a few steps, stumbled, righted herself, and took a few more. Then she held out her arms and twirled. "Now I'm a proper ballerina."

"You're a silly bird, is what you are." Eider mussed up her hair. "Let's go."

Holding hands, they began to walk again. Sisters marching side by side, headed Beyond. Where maybe they would even find a family.

Somewhere in the back of her mind, Eider knew it couldn't be that easy. She was nine years old, after all. Not six. But hope can be very convincing.

Even in the middle of the desert.

It grew hotter, as deserts do. To keep their minds off the heat, the girls talked about different types of families they'd read about in books. "A dad and a mom, or two moms, or only a single grandfather," Eider said. "No sisters, or ten sisters, or three identical brothers. A cat or a dog—"

"No dog," Robin said.

"Not all dogs are mean dogs."

"No dog!"

Eider chuckled. Robin hated the Handyman's dog. "Fine, no dog. How about a fox? A little kit fox—they're not scary at all."

Robin giggled. "I like foxes."

"We'll live in a real house," Eider said. "With a front door and a yard in the back. Maybe a house in a forest. Or on a mountain."

"Or by the sea."

"A house by the sea! We can sit on the porch with our family and watch mermaids combing their hair in the huge, crashing waves."

Robin sighed dreamily. "Sounds perfect."

Eider sighed too. It made her realize how dry her mouth was. They'd packed two bottles of water each, which had seemed like a lot back at the ranch. Not anymore. Especially as the sun arced higher and higher in the sky.

They walked more. And spoke less.

At the hottest part of the day, the girls found an outcrop of rock and rested in its shade. Robin finished her first bottle of water, her cheeks bright pink. Eider hoped she wasn't sunburned. "If Teacher was here, she'd tell us to get out of the sun."

"I don't like Teacher," Robin said.

"Robin!" Eider exclaimed.

"Do you?"

"Sure. I mean, I don't know. I've never really thought about it."

Teacher was their guardian. She'd always been there, like the desert ranch. She was all they knew. And all they had.

Somewhere not too far off, a dog barked. Or maybe it was a coyote. "You'd never discipline me," Robin said. "No matter how bad I got."

"Of course I wouldn't. Even if I knew what discipline was," Eider joked.

Robin didn't smile.

The breeze picked up, and sand tickled their legs. Eider wanted to change the subject. "Do you think it's cool enough to keep walking? The shadows are longer now."

Which meant night was coming, she realized. They didn't have long before the dark. Eider hadn't really considered being out here at night. Or where they'd spend it. It was inevitable, though. No matter how quickly they walked, how fast they raced, the night would catch up.

And Teacher would too.

The truth was, Eider hadn't considered much at all. Running away had always seemed like a fantasy, even after they'd set out. Now, here they were, in the harsh reality of the desert Beyond. With night coming. And not much water left. And the horizon seemed just as far away as it had that morning.

The dog barked again. Eider hoped no wild animals would surprise them in the dark. She stood, then helped Robin to her feet. As she did, she caught sight of the ballet slippers—the silliest things to journey across the desert in. What if a scorpion stung her? Or a rattlesnake bit her? So many bad things could happen.

But a rattlesnake bite was just the beginning.

⸻

They'd walked another hour. Eider thought the landscape was starting to change. It seemed flatter the way they were headed. Less dry brush poking up, and more cricket song. A shimmer in the evening air.

Wait—a shimmer? Eider's heart rattled so loud, she thought she could hear it. "Hey," she began. "Do you think—"

And then, pain.

The first pain, anyway: needles. Twin quick, sharp stabs. But that first pain was nothing compared to the second pain. It rocketed from her ankle upward, though her leg, punching her stomach, choking her heart.

Robin's scream kept going. "It bit you! It bit you!"

Eider couldn't speak. She could only whimper as her pain grew worse and worse. Third pain, fourth, fifth.

"What do we do?" Robin cried. "What do we do?"

In the blur of her agony, Eider heard the dog bark again.

Woofwoofwoofwoofwoof

She recognized that bark—it was the Handyman's dog. "They're coming. They found us."

"Can they help you?"

Eider nodded. Nurse had snakebite medicine, and other kinds, too. But she didn't feel any relief at that thought. It was hard to feel anything through the pain.

"But they'll take us back," Robin said. "Will we be in trouble?"

Eider hadn't let herself truly consider it: getting caught. It would have ruined the fantasy. But now she had to face it. They'd be in trouble—so much trouble. They'd both be disciplined. And it was all Eider's fault.

"I don't want to go back," Robin said.

Eider squinted at her through pain-blurred eyes. "Robin . . ."

"I won't."

"You can't stay out here alone."

"I'll find a family. Like you said."

"But—"

"I can do it, Eider. If there's something out there."

Eider's head felt so woozy, her eyes glazed with fog. Robin swam in and out, her stubborn feet planted, her blackbird hair in her face.

"Is there?" she asked.

"There . . . there has to be." Eider didn't know if it was a lie or not.

"Then I'll find it."

"Take my bag," she whispered. "Keep walking west. Straight west—toward where the sun goes down. Away from the night."

"West," Robin repeated.

"And—don't say anything. To anyone. Not a word, until I come find you. I promise I'll find you. Wherever you are."

Robin's eyes spilled over. "You'll be okay?"

"I'll be okay." Maybe the truth, maybe a lie. "As long as you are."

The sisters embraced, Robin's wet, warm cheek pressed against Eider's. And then a sudden chill as Robin pulled away. She darted toward a pleat in the desert sameness, like she'd been eyeing it the whole time.

A blackbird hop and she was gone.

As Eider heard the van crunch closer, she closed her eyes. Her head panged. Her leg felt like it didn't belong to her, a hot white agony of pain. It made her thoughts spiral and spin, entirely nonsensical. Like the notion that she'd just let her six-year-old sister run away into the desert night wearing nothing but overalls and ballet slippers.

Alone.

But that was crazy. It couldn't be true. Eider's last thought before she passed out: that she'd made a mistake.

The biggest mistake of her life.

—

Eider remembered dreaming.

Most of her dreams had sharp, jagged edges. A beach house crashing into the sea. A purple coyote with sharp teeth. A man with a trout for a head. A copper braid that wrapped around her ankles, sending her tumbling.

She remembered pain that spiked and burned. Pain in her ankle. Pain in her head. Pain in her heart.

She remembered Nurse spoon-feeding her soup, but she didn't taste any stars.

Mostly, she remembered sleeping. Sleeping and sleeping and sleeping. When the fever broke at long last, Teacher and Nurse were both beside her bed. They weren't looking her way, but when she croaked, they turned.

"Welcome to the land of the living!" Nurse said.

"We were very worried about you," Teacher said. "How are you feeling?"

Eider's ankle, head, and heart throbbed all at once. "What about Robin?" she asked in reply. She cared about nothing else.

"Robin?" Teacher repeated. A question.

"Did you find her?"

"Did we find who?"

"Robin!" Eider said. What was going on? "Where is she?"

Nurse looked distressed. "Oh dear," he said. "Why don't you get some more rest, kiddo? Clearly, you're still unwell."

"Not until you tell me what happened to my sister!"

"Eider . . ." Teacher tipped her head one way, then the other. "You don't have a sister."

—

Weeks passed before Eider felt ready to visit the cement slabs alone. Not just because of the alone part—all the new structure stalled her, too. All the new rules.

Everything had a set schedule now. A time and a place. They had little time for hobbies like tinkering, drawing, even dancing—which didn't matter much, since Eider's ballet shoes were gone. Along with any mention of Robin. Whenever Eider said her sister's name, the other kids ignored her, changed the subject, or worse. She'd never felt more alone.

And in the classroom, where rows of bookshelves had once stood, now there was only one. "What's going on?" Finch asked.

"Don't speak unless you're called on," Teacher said sharply.

Finch looked stunned.

"I used to think I should share as much from Before as possible. To let in everything I possibly could: all the storms, and all the sunlight, too. But by opening those windows, I allowed your minds to meander, instead of focus."

Teacher set the very first World Book in the middle of the table. "From now on, lessons will be structured around these books, starting with A."

Eider didn't even look at it. She was too busy drowning in the empty space where a chair had never been.

That night, her loneliness turned to restlessness. She made sure Avis and Linnet were asleep. She checked that Teacher's lights were off. Nurse's, too. It felt like a whole lot of effort, when her only intention was to think. But she didn't want to get in trouble.

As Eider approached the slabs, she noticed something sitting on top of one of them. An odd-shaped lump in the dark. She hurried closer, barely daring to hope.

It was her fairytale book.

Heaped with dust, like it'd been there a long time. Since whenever Eider had last read it, before she and—

Before *Eider* had run away.

She shook off all the dust, then stuffed the book inside her overalls. She needed to hide it. Somewhere good—somewhere Teacher would never find it. The date grove? The storage room? She didn't know, but it was a spark of hope in a desert gone dark. A light that would comfort her through three years of night. Missing a sister who'd never existed.

22 MEMORIES THAT WERE

BUT **R**OBIN *HAD* EXISTED.

Eider knew that now. Linnet had stirred up the memories that were always there, just beneath the surface. Like stars in her soup. Eider had always pushed them back, her memories-that-were. But not anymore—and never again.

Robin had been real.

Which meant that she still was.

23
LIES

TEACHER HADN'T JUST HIDDEN THE TRUTH THIS TIME.

She'd lied. *On purpose.*

And not only Teacher, but Nurse and the other kids, too.

Eider thought of all the times she'd brought up Robin over the years. Deliberately, or accidentally. And the times the other kids had brought her up themselves. Even recently: like Jay, who'd been so awful about it. And Avis, too! It was even meaner now, in retrospect. So mean it took Eider's breath away.

For three years, the other kids had shared a secret with Teacher that Eider wasn't in on. But *why?* Why had they gone along with it? Because Teacher had told them to? Or had they somehow forgotten Robin had been real? Had their brains been pinched and prodded, like Eider's—just more successfully?

Eider didn't know. She felt more alone than ever.

Alone—but also relieved.

A great weight had lifted from her shoulders. A desert's worth of dust and wind. As she left the trailer the next morning, she tilted back her tear-streaked face and felt the sunshine on her skin. Sunshine, and starlight, too. Because the sun was a star, wasn't it? She reached for the sky with both arms. The sky, and the world Beyond.

Where all this time, Robin had been waiting to reach back.

—

Eider barely spoke to anyone the next few days. Not even to Linnet, though she slipped her a quiet smile or two.

She wanted to, though. She wanted to poke Finch so hard he yelped, grab Avis by her remaining hair, bash Jay over the head with his coyote skull. Call them liars, every last one of them. Nurse and Teacher, too. Teacher, the most.

But she didn't.

She kept trying at lessons. She cared less than ever, but she didn't want Teacher to notice the change in her. The wheels in her head that had started to turn. The light peeking through after years of cloud cover.

Teacher had been hiding the truth—now, Eider knew that for sure. And not only about the reality of Robin. But why? All those lies had to have a point. If Teacher was hiding something else from them, something *more* . . . where would she keep it?

Eider was pretty sure she knew the answer: Teacher's office.

Though Eider was intrigued by off-limits places, she'd never found it that interesting. Maybe because Teacher had never made it sound particularly exciting. "Work, work, work," she'd say before heading over.

But what kind of work? Lesson planning couldn't account for all the time Teacher spent there, especially lately. What other work did she do? What was in there, anyway? Delicious food? Narwhals and puffins and automobiles? Secret papers? Books?

Books.

The books were in Teacher's office! They had to be. All the books Teacher had taken away three years ago. Unless she'd burned them, like Finch's notebooks. But even if Eider found the books, what would that prove? The other kids already knew Teacher had taken them.

The office must hold some other kind of evidence. Some other proof of Teacher's lies. If Eider was going to find it, she needed help.

But who could she trust?

Linnet had been so brave, telling Eider the truth about Robin. But she was far too timid to help with something this risky. Eider sure wasn't about to ask Jay. And she couldn't ask Finch, not after he'd been disciplined.

Then there was Avis.

Avis, who'd lied about Robin, like everybody else. Lied while brushing and braiding Eider's hair. Lied while Eider shared her secret thoughts about Beyond and Before. Lied and lied and lied.

But she'd been there for Eider after her fever. She stood up for Eider whenever Jay teased her. A couple times, she'd even let Eider read her a story.

Avis was Eider's best friend.

If Eider couldn't rely on her, what was the point of having a best friend at all?

—

During Free Play, Eider found Avis behind the classroom, flipping through a stack of mind-reading cards.

The sight made Eider pause. Avis had never been the type to study outside of lessons. Eider watched her pick a card and squint at the back. Jot something in her notebook, then flip the card over. "Darn it," she muttered.

"Avis," Eider said.

Avis glanced up. "Oh," she said, looking embarrassed. Quickly, she straightened the stack of cards and wrapped a rubber band around them. "I was just goofing around."

Eider waved her hand. "I don't care. We need to talk."

"About what? I'm kind of busy. . . ."

"Busy goofing around?" Eider raised her eyebrows. "I

really need to talk to you. It's serious. Very serious. Can we go to the date grove?"

"I don't like it there. There's spiders."

"There are spiders everywhere, Avis. Come on."

"Can't we talk right here?"

Eider exhaled, a little storm of frustration. Already, Avis was making this hard for her. But then again, hadn't she always? Anytime Eider brought up a serious topic, Avis acted annoyed or changed the subject. "Please, Avis?"

Avis sighed. *"Fine."*

Minutes later, they stood in the shade of the date grove. A breeze ruffled the palm fronds, and a bird trilled softly overhead.

"So what is this about?" Avis asked haughtily. "Because—"

"You lied to me."

"No I didn't. About what?"

"About . . ." Eider took a deep breath. "About Robin."

Avis rolled her eyes. "Eider! You're talking crazy again. You know she doesn't—"

"Yes, she does. Linnet told me the truth."

"Linnet?" Avis tried to roll her eyes again, but they didn't quite make it. "She doesn't know—she's probably confused. . . ."

"Stop lying to me, Avis!"

Eider yelled it in her best friend's face. She hadn't even meant to—it just came out. All those months and years swallowing it down. All that time calling Avis her best friend, and Avis agreeing.

Avis's haughty expression started to slip. And then it crumpled.

"Eider, I'm sorry," she said, her voice breaking. "Teacher told us to. She *made* us."

"Made you how?"

"She said it was the only way to make sure you got well. That you couldn't move forward with your feet stuck in the past. You were sick in the head."

"I was sick with a rattlesnake bite!"

"But it made you crazy. Do you know the things you said? Real crazy stuff—not just about Robin. About talking foxes, and mermaids, and people who came from the stars. And you kept crying out for her. All day and all night. We were so worried about you, Eider. It made us feel crazy, too."

Eider paused. "I didn't realize . . ."

"Of course you didn't realize. You still don't—that it wasn't only *you* who had to move on. It was all of us. Because Robin wasn't just yours."

"What do you mean?"

"That we all missed her, Eider!" Avis was crying now. "We were all scared and sad. Not as much as you, of course, I'm not saying that. I know how close you were. I was jealous of you two. We've never been as close."

"Yeah, but . . . she was my sister."

"That doesn't matter."

Eider didn't want to argue. "It's just . . . Robin looked at stuff the same way as me, you know? Outward instead of inward. You never want to—you hate it when I do."

"Because we're not supposed to."

"Says who?"

"Teacher."

Eider reached out and grabbed Avis's hand. "That's the thing," she said. "Don't you see? Teacher is the one who started the lie in the first place. She made you lie to me. Why should we trust her? Why should we keep doing what she says?"

Avis pulled her hand away. "Eider!"

"You know she's lied about other stuff. You know it. I met somebody, Avis! A hiker, when I was out exploring. He had blue shoes for walking far. And a thing with magic moving pictures on it."

"Magic moving *what*? What are you even talking about?"

Eider knew she was sounding crazy again, even though she was telling the truth. "Never mind. I'll explain later. But I need to know what else Teacher is lying about. *We* need to know. Will you help me, Avis?"

"I don't want to get in trouble again." Avis sniffled.

"It'll be worth it. I swear." Eider took a deep breath, then explained the plan she'd come up with. Avis's eyes alternately widened and narrowed, widened and narrowed. And then they stayed narrowed.

"Eider . . ." she said.

Eider leaned in, but she didn't yell this time. She spoke firmly. The way Teacher did when she gave orders. "You owe me this, Avis. Are you my best friend, or not?"

"Yeah! But best friends don't get other friends in trouble."

"We won't get in trouble," Eider said. "As long as you help me."

She hoped she sounded more confident than she felt. Which wasn't particularly confident at all.

ALL EIDER NEEDED TO DO WAS WAIT FOR A DRILL.

Drills could come at any time, from dawn until dusk or dusk until dawn. Eider had to be prepared at every moment. Listening with her fingers. Looking with her nose. Feeling with her eyes.

Extrasensory lessons had really paid off. When the alarm finally sounded a few days later, Eider was ready.

Eeeeee. Eeeeee. Eeeeee.

They'd just sat down in the dining area for lunch (lumpy lentil soup, yuck). Everybody groaned except Eider and Avis. Jay scooped up his bowl and mug. "I'm taking these with me."

Avis had avoided Eider's eyes ever since their conversation at the date grove. But now, she grabbed Eider's arm.

"What do we do if Nurse comes in and you're not back yet?"

"Nothing," Eider whispered. "Do nothing. It's not like he counts us—he just sticks his head inside."

"But what if Teacher opens the door? She'd notice you were gone for sure."

"I don't know, make something up."

"Or what if—what if the danger really is real this time?"

That made Eider pause. Teacher had never specified what kind of dangers they were hiding from, exactly. And Eider had never seen any sign of danger. No changes in the desert sameness.

But then again . . .

"It'll be okay," Eider said. "Just go!"

Avis ran for the shelter.

Eider ran in the opposite direction.

—

With the alarm screaming in Eider's ears, the cement slabs seemed farther than ever. It almost felt like she was in a real war, running for cover. Except cover was the other way.

Somehow, she made it. She crouched beside one of the slabs, angling her head so it didn't show over the top. She was glad for her dark hair. Avis's rusty-red locks would have stood out like a bright bandana.

When the alarm stopped, Eider counted to one hundred. Another fifty for good measure. Then, ever so carefully, she lifted her head and peered over the edge of the slab.

Everything looked the same. The desert ranch, and the desert sameness that surrounded it. Then she spotted a bit of movement.

Teacher, at the gate—unlocking the padlock.

The van waited nearby, with Nurse in the driver's seat. As Eider watched, he drove through the open gate. Teacher locked the gate and then climbed inside the van. It started moving again, its knobby tires crunching into the open desert.

Eider watched the van grow smaller and smaller, until it dipped below the horizon and vanished. She rubbed her eyes, but the van was still gone.

Teacher and Nurse were gone.

Was this always what happened during drills? Eider wondered. Teacher and Nurse leaving the kids all alone? But *why*? Where was there to go?

And how long would they be gone? Right now, that question was the most important. Even if drills usually lasted for hours, Eider couldn't know for sure. She jumped to her feet and started sprinting for Teacher's office.

This would be a good time to run away.

The thought made her stumble. Did she really want to run away, after what had happened last time? Was she brave enough? She had been, once. But now she knew so much more. It seemed like the older you got and the more you learned, the less brave you became.

Either way, Eider refused to leave the other kids behind. Not until they'd all learned the truth about Teacher's lies.

As she hurried past, she couldn't help glancing at the spike's rusty sign:

NO TRESPASSING
KEEP OUT

The door to the office was locked, of course. What about windows? Eider could use a rock to bash one open, but then the break-in would be obvious.

She moved from window to window, each shrouded with curtains. One was open an inch but wouldn't budge any higher. The next had an even smaller opening—but it was large enough to wedge her fingertips underneath. She yanked and it opened wider. Her searching fingers found a latch.

The window opened all the way.

Eider wasn't the strongest kid at the desert ranch. But she was strong enough to hoist herself up and through the window.

Biting her thumbnail, she looked around Teacher's office.

She saw folders and binders organized in perfect stacks.

The breeze from a swamp cooler ruffled the papers. There was a table covered in strange machinery, including Finch's broken radio. An uncomfortable-looking chair. Everything was coated in a thin layer of dust, since the desert always found its way inside.

Then she saw the bookcase. On the top shelf sat the four World Books they hadn't gotten to yet: So–Sz, T, U–V, WXYZ.

And on the shelves below the World Books, more books. Dozens and dozens of books. *Their* books, just as Eider had expected. Her fingers grazed the spines she still recognized: *Astronomy: A History*, *Animalia*, *The Red Badge of Courage*, *Ballet Shoes*, *Star Wars Treasury*, *The Way Things Work*.

Eider wanted to reread them all. This time, she'd memorize them, like her windborne papers. Back then, she hadn't known what she'd soon be missing.

Or what she'd always been missing, because of Teacher.

The World Book contained many things, but it wasn't everything. It was only information. No memories attached. No stories. No people! They'd already lost the whole world. Why had Teacher taken so much else away?

Angry now, Eider grabbed the closest folder and flipped it open. Inside, there was a stack of pages. She recognized the old-timey letters on the top page:

TELEVISION

The pages were from the World Book. Teacher had taken them, too.

With the evidence finally in front of her, Eider's anger grew and grew. She wanted to steal the entire folder, but she knew Teacher might notice. So she drew three pages at random, folded them, and stuffed them in her overalls pocket.

Then she opened one of the binders. She was greeted by Teacher's all-caps handwriting. Paragraph after paragraph. Paper after paper. Binder after binder.

Was this why Teacher had been so busy lately? Eider kept flipping pages, mesmerized. Sometimes the letters grew in size, darting across the paper like angry insects. They became sloppier, and harder to read. Certain phrases still jumped out at her, the way they had during the radio broadcast:

HARNESSING POWERS

THE SPECIAL ONES

ONLY THE RIGHTEOUS WILL PREVAIL

THE END IS VERY NEAR

Eider's hands began to tremble. She closed the binder, then turned to face Teacher's strange machinery. She had no better name for it. Just an assemblage of wires, dials, switches, and speakers. Like Finch's radio, but bigger.

Like a great big radio.

Eider looked more closely. She saw a microphone—she'd read about them in World Book M. The Music section, which Teacher hadn't removed.

Her heart pounded. Microphones were for talking into. They made your voice louder. They amplified what you said, so others could hear it—if they were sitting in front of you. Or far away, maybe. If you wanted to broadcast your voice.

BECAUSE THE END IS VERY NEAR.
UNLESS . . . NOBODY WILL BE SAFE.
. . . THE SPECIAL ONES. WHEN THE DANGER ARRIVES . . .

"It was Teacher," Eider said. "The whole time."

Suddenly, her knees stopped working. She collapsed into Teacher's chair, which was even more uncomfortable than it looked.

No wonder the voice on the radio had sounded familiar. It'd been Teacher's voice, with ants running through it. Teacher, talking about the end of the world. They hadn't been hearing Other People—they'd been hearing Teacher.

But that meant Teacher had been *talking to* Other People.

Eider had thought plenty about the people broadcasting. She'd never considered the people listening. Gathered around radios of their own.

Maybe even right now.

She flipped the switch at the base of the microphone. A red light came on. She leaned forward until her mouth was an inch from the dusty black metal.

"Hello," she mouthed without any sound. "I am at the desert ranch. . . ."

"Anybody out there?" she mouthed.

"I'm right here," she mouthed. "I exist."

She cleared her throat to speak for real. But . . . what if Teacher had her own radio? What if she was listening this minute?

A flash of fear stabbed Eider's middle. She stood so quickly, the chair fell over with a clatter. She backed into the bookcase, terrified the sound would summon Teacher. But nothing happened. Because Teacher was far away.

When Eider could breathe again, she bent down to right the toppled chair. As she stood, she noticed a framed photo on Teacher's desk.

The frame was shimmery silver. There were people in the photo: a family. A kid and two parents. Eider didn't know the man parent.

But the woman parent was Teacher.

Astonished, Eider leaned in closer. The photo was very old, it seemed. Teacher's hair had color to it, and her face was unlined. But it was definitely Teacher.

Had Teacher had a *family*?

It didn't make any sense. None at all. And yet . . .

Eider shook her head, so overwhelmed she could barely

think. But she knew she had to leave. She paused long enough to switch off the microphone, and to lock the office door behind her.

Then she ran for the shelter.

ONLY HERE

Eɪᴅᴇʀ ʜᴀᴍᴍᴇʀᴇᴅ ʙᴏᴛʜ ꜰɪꜱᴛꜱ ᴏɴ ᴛʜᴇ ꜱʜᴇʟᴛᴇʀ ᴅᴏᴏʀ. From inside, she heard nothing. Her frantic pounding was probably scaring the other kids to bits.

"It's me," she said. She glanced over her shoulder—no sign of the van. The gate was still closed and locked. She raised her voice. "It's Eider!"

Nothing.

"You guys, the danger isn't real! Nobody's out here but me. Teacher and Nurse drove away in the van."

Still nothing. How much time did she have left? Then she heard voices inside. After another moment, the door opened a crack.

It was Jay. "You're okay!" he said.

Eider was startled by the relief in his voice. "Yes," she said. "No—I'm not. I mean, I'm not hurt. But I need to talk to you guys. I need to show you what I found."

Avis shoved Jay aside. "Where?"

"In Teacher's office."

There was a collective gasp from inside the shelter. "You were in Teacher's office?" Avis exclaimed. Eider couldn't help pausing a moment to glare. Avis had known the whole plan, after all—she'd even been part of it.

"What did you find?" Finch asked.

Eider slipped inside the shelter and closed the door behind her. After being alone outside, she felt claustrophobic in the small, confined space. "I found . . ." She took a deep breath to calm her racing heart. "I found a microphone."

Everybody stared at her. "So?" Jay said.

Eider ignored him, staring right at Finch. "And other stuff. Broadcasting stuff. The voice on the radio—it was Teacher."

Finch's expression showed only disbelief. "I don't think . . ." Then he paused, realization slowly dawning on his face. "An antenna."

"Huh?"

"The spike. It's an antenna."

"Like on a bug?" Jay asked.

"What? No, not like on a bug. An antenna for sending out radio signals. I can't believe I never realized it before."

"That's why she was so angry about your radio," Eider said. "She wasn't worried about us getting messages from Beyond. She was worried about us hearing her. You know she lies to us—"

"To *you*," Avis interrupted.

"If she'd lie to me, she'd lie to you too. And she *has*. She's lied to all of us—and I have proof right here." Eider pulled out the World Book pages and unfolded them. "They were in a folder in Teacher's office. Every single page she removed, I'll bet."

"Why are you so sure they were removed?" Avis asked. "How do you know they didn't just fall out or something?"

"They didn't just fall out. They were taken out on purpose. Look at them."

"*Adoption*?" Linnet read. "What's that?"

"I'm not sure," Eider said, "but look: *Siblings*. That's brothers and sisters. Teacher didn't like us to talk about those. And *War*! The first page of it, anyway. We haven't gotten to World Book W, but of course that section would be missing. . . ."

"What are you saying?" Avis asked.

"I'm saying Teacher removed the pages on purpose. She wants to control what we learn and what we don't learn. What we know and what we don't know. Like our old books—they were there, too."

"All the books?" Finch asked.

"Yep. She took them away. Just like—just like Robin."

Jay laughed, a little too loudly. "You know Robin wasn't—"

"Stop it, Jay!" Linnet exclaimed. "Robin was real. You know she was real. We all know."

Tears filled Eider's eyes as she glanced around the circle. Slight nods from everyone. First Linnet and Finch. Then Avis. And finally, Jay.

"So you've known this whole time," Eider said. "That Teacher lies. That she keeps things from us."

"From *you*," Avis said.

"Avis! Think! Why would Teacher and Nurse keep things from me and not the rest of you? Why am I so special—or not special?"

Nobody had an answer. They were all special. They were all not special. The same way they'd always been.

"But *why*?" Linnet asked. "Why would Teacher lie to us?"

"Because . . ." Eider began.

Everybody was staring at her. She stared back, glanced from kid to kid, the same way Teacher did. Finch's hair looked even paler. Linnet's cheeks were wet with tears. Jay's big shoulders heaved with emotion. Avis's expression was hard to read, but she looked scared. They all did.

And that's when Eider said it. Her most secret hope—her biggest fear. She stood up straight, took a deep breath, and said it out loud.

"Because the world hasn't ended."

Linnet gasped.

"Huh?" Jay said. "What?"

"What do you mean?" Finch said.

"Teacher told us the world's ended everywhere but the

desert ranch," Eider explained. "But it's the opposite. The world hasn't ended anywhere else. Only here."

She considered opening the shelter door and dramatically sweeping her hands across the desert sameness. But it probably wasn't the smartest idea right now.

"How do we know for sure?" Finch asked.

Eider liked that he'd said "we." "It's the only explanation that makes sense. The more you think about it—"

"No it doesn't," Avis interrupted. "It doesn't make any sense at all. Why lie to us about something so huge like that? For our whole entire lives? Why keep us here if the world still exists, with all the good stuff in it? What's the point?"

"I don't—"

"And why train us to be leaders? Why all these lessons, especially Extrasensory? All that talk about us being special? And our abilities? Are you saying Teacher's been lying about that too?"

"I don't think Teacher is lying about everything, necessarily," Eider said. "I think . . . she does want us to be leaders. But leaders who listen to her. Leaders who do what she wants."

There was a moment of silence.

"What do we do?" Linnet asked softly.

All of a sudden, Eider felt weary. She collapsed onto a cushion, her back against the shelter wall. "I don't know," she said. "I don't know."

By the time Nurse opened the door, the crickets were beginning to sing. "Top o' the evening to you, kiddos," he said. "Just a drill. Nothing to worry about."

Nobody said anything.

"Bobcat got your tongues?" Nurse waited a moment longer, then squinted at them. "Well, now you've got me worried. Is anything the matter?"

Linnet spoke up before Eider could. "We're just tired."

"Ah." Nurse nodded. "Drills are enough to make any-body tired. But they're so very important."

"Where do you go during drills, anyway?" Jay asked. "You and Teacher?"

Eider looked at him sharply. But Nurse just chuckled. "What do you mean?" he said. "We don't go anywhere."

"I just mean, how do you stay safe? If there's a danger, but you're not in the shelter with us?"

"Don't worry about us, silly goose." He patted Jay's head. "How about we get some dinner in you, kiddos? Dou-ble portions, since you skipped your lunch. Then you can scamper off to bed for some quality slumber."

Eider hadn't expected a better answer than that, but it angered her just the same. She saw the same feeling reflected in the other kids' eyes.

As they headed back to the dining area, Eider trailed behind. She hadn't eaten since lunch, but she wasn't hungry.

All of a sudden, she heard a rustling.

A white bird flew overhead. It had a curved neck, a hooked beak, and broad white wings. It flew in silence, but Eider could still hear it: the whisper of wind under its feathers, lifting it through the sky.

She tipped back her head to watch it. Where was it going? Had it come from the sea? The dead sea Eider had seen? The memory seemed so far away now, like an illustration in her fairytale book. Almost as far away as Robin.

But one thing was certain: The bird had come from Beyond. And Beyond was where it was headed.

Eider squinched her eyes shut. Breathed in, breathed out. She imagined what it would feel like to lift up, spread her wings, and ride the wind. To soar. Not the way Teacher meant, but literally.

All she had were her feet.

She opened her eyes and looked at them.

—

Eider had told the other kids to meet at the slabs that night. She hadn't known who would come, though. Maybe Finch. Or Jay, who never wanted anyone to think he was scared.

But they'd all come. Every single one.

The five of them sat atop the same slab, legs crossed, looking inward. Teacher would have liked that, Eider thought.

"What could we possibly do?" Avis was asking.

"How about using Teacher's broadcasting equipment?" Finch suggested. "Maybe we could break back in and broadcast a message—"

"How would we know anybody heard it, though?" Eider asked.

Avis rested her elbow on Jay's shoulder. He blushed instantly. "Worse," she said, "what if we got caught?"

Finch shrugged. "Anything's going to have some risk."

"Maybe one of us could sneak into the van," Jay said, trying to rub the pink from his cheeks. "Lie down in the backseat and wait. And then, whenever it stops, climb out and run."

"But it could take forever for them to drive anywhere," Finch said. "You might suffocate. Or get heatstroke."

Jay frowned. "I didn't say *me*."

"And anyway, run to where?" Avis asked. "And how would we get back, if we found some sort of help? Does anybody know *where* we actually are?"

"Camp Douglas," Eider said.

"Huh?" Avis said.

"Never mind. But we're not that far from the sea."

"If we were so close, wouldn't we smell it?"

"I think I do, sometimes," Linnet said.

Eider turned to her. "You do?"

Linnet nodded shyly, and Eider smiled. She wished she'd given the younger girl's friendship more of a chance. They'd had so much time, tucked away from the world. Locked away.

Linnet didn't deserve that. Robin hadn't, either. None of them did.

"I'll run away and get help," Eider said. "Myself."

Four pairs of eyes stared at her.

"How?" Jay asked. "In the van?"

"On foot."

"But what about rattlesnakes?" Linnet asked.

"I'll be careful. Much more careful than last time. . . ."

The other kids tried to talk Eider out of it. But it was the best plan they had. Eider had ventured Beyond the fence—not once, but many times. She'd been all the way to the sea. Most importantly, she had determination.

And, like one of Finch's grins, it spread.

Even after they had finished planning, the kids remained at the slabs for hours. Discussing where they'd go, if the whole wide world existed. What they'd do when they got there. What delicious things they'd eat and drink. Who they'd become. They talked until the first gray light of dawn brightened the horizon—the very same horizon Eider and Robin had set out to find, years ago, before their world had ended.

When the kids finally crept back to their trailers, Eider couldn't help noticing the look on Avis's face. Avis didn't really believe it. Not only about Teacher's lies. But that Eider was going to go at all.

It didn't matter. Eider believed in herself.

She believed in Robin.

And she believed in the other kids, too.

26

CHOICES

EIDER HAD JUST DRIFTED OFF when she woke to banging. At first, she thought it was the Handyman again, patching up another part of the fence.

Bang. Bang. Bang.

Except this sound was way too close.

Then a voice: "You have ten seconds."

Eider sat up in bed, blinking. Ten seconds until what? In their own beds, Avis and Linnet looked just as bewildered.

The door opened. "Put on your boots and come outside," Teacher said.

The three girls glanced at each other, then scrambled to pull on their boots. Eider swallowed hard. What was going on? Did Teacher know they'd met last night? Had one of the boys told on them?

Outside, the desert sameness was the delicate pink of

sunrise. The wind had picked up since they'd gone to bed. Teacher stood next to the Handyman, the mean dog bouncing frantically on the other end of his leash.

Woofwoofwoofwoofwoof

"Look for anything out of the ordinary," Teacher told the Handyman. "Anything that clearly doesn't belong to them."

The Handyman looped the mean dog's leash around the door handle. Then he disappeared inside their trailer. Right away, they heard banging and thumping, like all their belongings were being overturned.

Teacher faced the girls. Her expression was unreadable, but her voice was edged in razors. "Go wait with the boys in the classroom. I'll join you in a minute."

Beside her, Eider felt Linnet tremble. She put an arm around her. "Let's go."

"But what if he finds it?" Linnet whispered as the girls hurried away. "The piece with the flowers?"

"The piece?" Eider repeated, Then she realized Linnet meant the ceramic shard. "Oh, Linnet. Don't worry. I'm sure that's not what they're looking for."

"Or the marker? I—"

"I'll bet she knows about her office," Avis said, stepping in front of them. "I'll bet you messed up something, and now we're all going to get in trouble."

"I didn't mess up anything!"

Eider knew she'd been careful, leaving everything just

as she'd found it. Except for the three World Book pages she'd taken, and there was no way Teacher could have noticed those. But then again—where were they?

The boys were already in the classroom, too nervous to sit. "Finch," Eider whispered urgently. "Where are the pages? Did you leave them in the trailer?"

Finch shook his head. "I—"

"Shhh!" Avis said. "She's coming."

Sometimes, Teacher looked old and weary. Like she carried the weight of the end of the world on her shoulders. Other times, she looked strong and commanding. Like every single word she said had the power to fill a room.

As she stepped through the door of the classroom, she was both. Weary. But powerful.

"I'm extremely disappointed in you all," she said. "Not just disappointed—I'm saddened. Ashamed. I told you how important it is not to sneak, not to keep secrets. I trusted you to tell me the truth. And you didn't.

"Does anybody have anything to say?"

All the kids were rigid, silent. Then came a knock at the door.

Rap. Rap. Rap.

"Come in," Teacher said.

Eider hoped it would be Nurse. His loopy presence seemed to defuse tense situations. But it was the Handyman, carrying a sack. At least he'd left the mean dog outside, though Eider could still hear it.

Woofwoofwoofwoofwoof

"Found a few things." The Handyman reached into the bag and pulled out a handful of dingy fabric scraps, dumping them on the table. "Inside the redhead's pillowcase."

"Those are just for hair," Avis protested.

He withdrew a wad of papers. "These belong to the quiet one."

Papers? Eider's stomach dropped—but these papers didn't belong to her. They were striped notebook pages, with drawings on them: animal faces, intricate designs, teeny tiny flowers like the ones on the shard. Many of them were in permanent marker.

Eider squeezed Linnet's hand.

The Handyman withdrew a few more handfuls of items: wires, old batteries, twists of metal. "These odds and ends in the skinny boy's cubby, stuffed behind his nightshirt." From the bottom of his sack, he pulled the biggest item of all. "This box under the big one's bed. Smells kind of rank."

"I kept telling him that," Finch muttered.

"Is that all?" Teacher asked the Handyman, who nodded. "Thanks for your help."

After the Handyman left, the room didn't feel any less crowded. Teacher looked inside Jay's box, then made a face.

"I can explain . . ." Jay began.

"I don't want to hear any excuses," Teacher said. "I just want to know what else you've been hiding. Everyone, empty your pockets." When the kids hesitated, she shouted, "Now!"

Everybody reached into the pockets of their nightshirts and turned them inside out. Finch, Avis, and Eider had nothing. Linnet placed her shard on the table with shaking hands. Jay pulled out the World Book pages. Eider squeezed her eyes shut.

"Where did you get those?" Teacher demanded.

"I don't . . ." Jay stammered. "I didn't . . ."

Teacher reached out to take the pages. But Jay held on, and they ripped in two. Jay winced and handed over the other halves.

"You broke into my office. What else did you take?"

Jay shook his head. "No! I—"

"Don't lie to me, Jay. You left the window open."

Eider's heart plummeted all the way to her toes. The window. She'd left the window open. How could she have been so stupid? She waited for Jay to tell on her. Of course he would—it was Jay, the meanest. But he just stood there, his big mouth shut.

Eider didn't feel relieved. She couldn't let anybody else take the blame. Not with so much on the line.

She stepped forward. "It wasn't Jay. It was me. I broke into your office."

Teacher stared at Eider. And then she laughed. Just a quick, short chuckle, but it frightened Eider even more than her raised voice.

"Why am I not surprised?" Teacher said. "It's always something with you, Eider. I think we're long past due for a little talk."

A little talk. The same thing Teacher had said to Avis and Finch, right before they were disciplined.

"I'll speak with the rest of you later. Pick up the mess in your trailers, and then get to studying. We have weeks and weeks of *S* to cover."

Eider bit her thumbnail as the other kids filtered out, glancing back at her over their shoulders. She tried to smile. She didn't want them to be scared for her.

———

Teacher stood at the other end of the classroom, facing Eider. The distance made her seem even more intimidating.

"Why did you break into my office, Eider?"

Eider began searching for an excuse. But then, what was the point of lying anymore? Maybe if she told the truth, she'd get the truth back. "Because . . ." She swallowed. "Because I know you've been lying to us."

"Oh?" Teacher said calmly.

"For our entire lives. Not just lying, but hiding the truth. About the whole world. About everything that's left. That's *still* left."

Eider couldn't believe she was talking to Teacher this way. But this was her chance. Except her words started coming out in a jumble.

"All the stuff you didn't want us to know about, you took away. The books and the World Book pages. The narwhals and the puffins. The birds all came from somewhere, and the Handyman, too. Because Finch's radio worked—we know you're broadcasting. It's all lies. Especially about—about—"

"Especially about what?"

"About Robin."

Teacher had just been standing there, listening. Looking mildly interested—even a little amused. Now she strode across the room, taking a seat that was way too close.

"Oh, Eider," she said. It was the voice she'd used when they were little, to soothe them. Eider couldn't remember the last time she'd heard it. "You're right that we've been hiding things. But don't you think we had reasons?"

"Reasons?"

"You just don't think. Only about yourself." Teacher sighed. "I was saving those World Book pages until you had enough background information to understand them. I was never planning on keeping them from you forever.

"And yes, we've been sending out radio broadcasts. As I've told you, most people out there are dangerous—which means all their radio broadcasts are, too. By putting out good messages, we're helping to dilute the dangerous ones. Helping the world begin again. The *right* way."

As always, Teacher had an answer for everything.

But something still didn't match up. "Okay," Eider began. "But what about everything else? You taught us the world has ended. That nothing's left—but it's not true. Why are we here if the world hasn't ended?"

"I'm keeping you safe," Teacher said. "I'm keeping all of you safe."

"From *what*?"

Teacher turned for a moment, as if to stare out the window. It made Eider think of the time she'd come across her brushing her hair, with her eyes in some faraway place. But this time, there wasn't any window. Only a wall.

"Do you know why you're here, Eider?"

"Because I'm brilliant," Eider said impatiently, "and special, whatever."

"Now you are. But you weren't when I found you."

Eider was dumbfounded. "You . . . found me?"

"I found all of you," Teacher said. "All of you were unwanted. Unloved. If I hadn't saved you—if *we* hadn't, Nurse and I—nobody would ever have known how special you are. You'd be like everyone else, wasting your life away. You never would have realized your potential."

"But—but we know it now," Eider said. "You've told us. Why are we still here? Why can't we just leave?"

"It's not that simple, Eider. It isn't safe."

"I don't care."

Teacher took a deep breath. She closed her eyes a couple beats, then opened them. "Maybe there is more world left than I led you to believe. But that doesn't mean it's a safe place to go back to. It's not like you think. It's not the world from your storybooks."

Eider narrowed her eyes. "You mean, the books you took away?"

"After you ran away, I had to. Don't you see? All those stories made you silly and naïve. They filled your head with imaginary creatures, fantasies of the sea, fairytale notions of *family*." Teacher scoffed. "That's not what the real world is like, Eider. It's dangerous. More dangerous than you could ever dream of. Maybe the world hasn't ended yet— but it's going to."

Eider remembered a fragment of Teacher's broadcast:

BECAUSE THE END IS VERY NEAR.

"It's—it's going to?" A knot of doubt twisted Eider's stomach.

"It has to. Think about it, Eider. Think about everything you've learned in the World Book. Even in your silly storybooks. I don't mean the lovely, thrilling things— whatever you feel you've missed out on. But the dangers. Murder. Wars. Famine. Tragedy.

"That's what the desert ranch is keeping you safe from. Before you were faced with harsh reality, we wanted to give you children a safe space to grow. To reach your full potential as the leaders you were born to be!"

Teacher's eyes were filled with fire and conviction. But Eider felt nothing but disbelief.

"It's not worth it," she said.

Teacher stood up. "Well, it's for your own good. The

five of you are just children, and we're your guardians. That's what guardians do: they protect children from making dangerous decisions."

But they didn't get to make *any* decisions, Eider thought. Let alone dangerous ones. "What if we'd make good decisions?"

"You wouldn't know any better. You proved that with Robin."

Teacher had said her name.

Eider felt it like a spark in her heart. But it didn't make her sad or ashamed like Teacher had intended it to—it just made her angry.

"Was that for my own good, too?" Eider's voice shook. "All the lies?"

"We didn't take it lightly. But we decided giving you a clean slate was best. If you could forget your sister—"

"I never forgot her!"

"Because you're just as stubborn as she was." Teacher shook her head. "Eider, we were trying to protect you. From grief, yes. But even more from that, from guilt."

Eider paused. "Guilt?"

"When you had the freedom to make choices, you made the wrong ones. You ran away into the desert. You left your little sister behind."

"But I . . . I didn't mean to."

"Whether you meant to or not, the damage was done."

Eider's anger had dulled to a painful ache. "That doesn't mean we couldn't have looked for her. . . ."

"We did look for her."

"You did?"

"Of course we did. We searched for days, but we couldn't find her."

Eider's heartbeat quickened. "So she made it!"

"Made it?" Teacher shook her head sadly. "I doubt it. That's a big, big desert out there."

Now Eider felt like her heart was escaping. She clutched it with both hands. "No . . ."

"I'm sorry, Eider. But Robin was a child. With a child's legs. The closest town is eighty miles west. Even the closest highway is a dozen miles away. With unimaginable dangers between. An adult couldn't make it across, let alone a child—"

"Charles made it."

For the first time in Eider's life, Teacher seemed caught completely off guard. "Who?"

"Charles the Hiker. I met him when I was exploring. He'd made it all the way out here. And he wasn't dangerous, like you said Other People are. He was a father. He had a family. He was good."

Teacher opened her mouth and closed it. The color had left her face. It made her look almost . . . *scared*.

But scared like a rattlesnake. Frozen, but tail still twitching. Dangerous in its fear.

"Do the other children know about this . . . Charles?"

Eider hesitated. She didn't know which was safer for her friends: a yes or a no. In her moment of hesitation, Teacher made a grab for her.

She bolted.

She threw herself across the classroom, pushing open the door before Teacher could catch her. Just as suddenly, she was flat on her back. The mean dog barked in her face, slobber splattering onto her cheeks.

"Down, boy," the Handyman said, and the dog slunk away.

"Let's take her to the shelter," Teacher said from the classroom doorway. "I don't trust this child, not for one second. I should have disciplined her a long time ago."

"So what?" Eider cried, reckless now. "Who cares? What else can you take away?"

"You have no idea," Teacher said.

She grabbed Eider's arm and hauled her to her feet. Eider tried to twist free, but it was no use. She was forced to follow Teacher. Like they always had.

They'd never had a choice at all.

27
DARKNESS

IN THE DAYTIME, THE SHELTER WAS DIM. But once the sun set, the darkness was complete.

Eider didn't have her penlight. All she had was her boots, her nightshirt, and herself. She sat against the door, hoping her eyes would adjust. But she was too scared to concentrate the way she'd been taught.

The wind outside didn't help. It coaxed up all kinds of sounds and swirled them together. It mixed up all the scents, too. For a moment, Eider thought she smelled the sea. Not the clear blue sea with huge, crashing waves. But the sulphury, dead-fish sea.

It made her chest tighten, remembering. The sea had been dead for real—just like Teacher had said.

But . . . maybe just that part of the sea was dead, not the whole thing. The sea was huge, wasn't it? So big it covered almost the entire world. The desert ranch, and the desert itself, was only one tiny speck of it. A planet in a universe of space.

But not empty space. Eider knew that now.

There was a whole wide world for her to see—and she was a prisoner here. Or maybe she'd always been a prisoner, but now she was even more trapped. Locked in the shelter from the outside.

What would happen to her?

The real world was dangerous, but Teacher was dangerous, too. The shelter wasn't a safe place. The desert ranch wasn't a safe place.

Maybe it had never been one.

—

Eider was still slumped against the door, half-asleep, when she heard the lock twist above her. She crawled away, scrambling to her feet right as it opened.

It was Jay.

He was the greatest thing she'd ever seen.

Behind him, the darkness was already lifting. It meant Eider had spent almost an entire day and night in the shelter. As if on cue, her stomach growled. "Where's—"

"Hurry up," Jay said, interrupting. "They're not paying attention. Linnet's throwing a tantrum. The way Robin used to."

"What's the matter?"

Jay exhaled loudly. "Nothing's the matter! She's distracting them."

"Really? Linnet?" Eider shook her head in amazement. "Wait—how'd you get the door open?"

"Teacher didn't take the Locks section." He held up a page from the World Book, torn out jaggedly. "Finch helped explain it."

"Why didn't he unlock the door himself?"

"He was busy unlocking Teacher's office. Now he's waiting at the slabs with your stuff. Are you gonna keep asking questions, or are you gonna go?"

Eider grinned. "You're all right, Jay."

Then she ran for the slabs.

All around her, the wind lifted milky beige dust into the sky. She avoided the rise and took the long way, past the date grove. The Handyman had fixed the fence, she remembered. She'd have to figure out a way to climb it—

A hand grabbed her arm. Eider almost yelled, then realized it was Avis. She must have been waiting in the trees.

"Don't go, Eider," Avis begged. Her shaggy red hair blew wildly around her face. "*Please*. You know how angry Teacher's going to be when she finds out. Remember what happened last time? Everything got so much worse."

"It'll be different this time," Eider said. "I won't let her find me."

"How do you know she won't? And even if you get

away, things will still be worse for the rest of us. You're being selfish."

"I won't let that happen, Avis. I'll find help."

"How can we trust that?"

"Because I'm me, not Teacher."

"I know, but . . ." Avis's eyes were wet. "I wish you wouldn't. Where are you going to go?"

"West. Toward the sea." Eider remembered what Teacher had said. *The closest town is eighty miles west.* "And the closest town."

Avis nodded. "Okay."

She reached out and squeezed Eider's hand. Then she turned and ran away.

Eider sprinted for the slabs. She didn't know if Avis had changed, or if she'd always been this person. Bold, but also scared. The way Linnet could be timid, but also brave. Jay could be trustworthy. Eider could be strong, and fast.

And Finch was smart—but not always. Like right now. He was hiding behind the slabs, but not quite enough. His hair practically glowed in the dark. "Are you okay?" he asked Eider.

She nodded. "Get down a little lower, will you?"

Finch crouched all the way down. "I grabbed your overalls and your jacket. And other things in a pack. Some cans of food and an opener. Two bottles of water."

It wouldn't be enough, Eider knew—she was already so thirsty. But it was better than nothing. "Wow! Thanks, Finch."

She crawled around the corner to change into her overalls. As she pulled them over her nightshirt, she felt something in the pocket—the housing-development pamphlet! Was that a sign?

"I promise I'll send help when I find it," Eider said as she tightened her boots. "I'll go as fast as I can—"

"I'm coming with you," Finch said.

"Really?"

"Of course. I wouldn't let you go alone. You're my best friend."

Eider almost felt like crying. "You're sure?" she asked, crawling back beside him. "They'll come after us."

"The others are going to keep distracting them. I took the rest of the World Book pages and all those important-looking papers in Teacher's binders, and I gave them to Jay." He grinned. "Too bad it's windy out, huh? It'll take an awfully long time for her to get them all back. . . ."

Eider grinned, too. "Let's go."

28
THE SEA THAT WASN'T

THE SEA WAS JUST LIKE EIDER REMEMBERED IT.

She had kept hoping she'd gotten her memory wrong. That the sea wasn't as bad as she recalled. Or that Teacher had led her to some rotten part of it, and the blue crashing part was just a little farther.

But just the like desert, the sea had a sameness all its own. The same patchy browns and muddy blues. The same fish-bone sand sinking their boots.

Then she saw the birds.

Five of them: great white birds, just like the one she'd seen soaring overhead. Not flying this time, but wading in the water on tall, skinny legs. The birds didn't seem to mind the ugly colors, or the stink in the air.

"Wow." Finch's eyes were huge. "I just can't believe this was in walking distance the whole time."

"A long walk," Eider said, since it had taken them all morning to get there. "But yeah."

As they watched, one of the tall white birds dipped its head in the water. It emerged with a live fish, flopping wildly in its beak.

Eider cried out. "There *are* real fish!"

"Obviously," Finch said. "I mean, the dead ones are still rotting. That means they were alive not that long ago."

She hadn't thought of that.

They walked farther along the water. It was still windy, though not as blustery as when they'd first set out. Eider imagined Teacher's papers blowing every which way, all across the desert ranch, maybe even Beyond, while Teacher and Nurse ran after them. Despite her nervousness, the image was silly enough to make her smile.

Before long, the beach began to widen. The fish bones hardened into dirt. Eider noticed tire marks, though she couldn't tell how old they were. She saw crunchy patches of grass. And trash everywhere, like the kind she'd found in the ravine. Bits of pipe. Broken wedges of plastic. Curls of wire.

Finch pocketed a few items, then pointed. "Hey, isn't that a table?"

They hurried over. It looked as ancient as the spotty sea. An end-of-the-world table, with twin benches attached.

"There's another one over there," Eider said. "And— what's that?"

Beside the second table stood a big metal cylinder, with

the word TRASH painted on it in bright red. It didn't look that ancient. Eider leaned over and peered inside, expecting nothing.

"Oh!" she exclaimed.

"What?" Finch said.

Eider reached inside the metal cylinder and withdrew a crumpled, colorful paper bag. "*Fast food*," she read. "What does that mean?"

Finch shrugged. "What kinds of food are fast?"

Eider uncrumpled the bag. Inside, she found a napkin and a yellow wrapper, greasy but empty. She could smell it, though: tart and strong. It made her mouth water.

"Smells like pickles," Finch said.

The bag still had some weight to it. She overturned it. A few fat foil packets fell into her hand. "*Tomato ketchup*," she read.

"That doesn't look like a tomato," Finch said.

Eider pinched off a corner of the foil packet. She sniffed, then brought the packet to her mouth and squeezed. The flavor pinched her tongue. "It doesn't taste like a tomato, either," she said, handing the packet to Finch.

He squeezed the rest into his mouth. "It's sour. And sweet. I think I like it."

She and Finch split the last two foil packets. Then they checked the other two trash cans. The stiff heel of bread they found tasted like the desert, but Eider didn't need food to be delicious.

They found a faucet, too. Or that's what Finch said it was. When he swiveled the handle, she expected nothing—but it worked! They finished the water in their bottles, then filled them, then drank and filled them again.

"Now what?" he asked.

Eider gazed out at the sea. At its scummy-looking patches. Stink waves, she thought. She'd told Robin to head west. But west was across the sea. How could they get there? Was it even possible?

"We need a boat," she said.

"Where are we going to get a boat?" Finch asked.

She glanced at the table. "Make one?"

"No way. How? We don't even have any tools."

Eider knew he was right. "But what else can we do?"

"Walk around it?"

"Around the entire sea?" She laughed incredulously. "That'd take a million years, Finch. The sea is *huge*. You know that just as well as I do."

"I don't think this is the sea."

She blinked at him. "Huh?"

"Not the ocean, anyway. Look really carefully, straight across." He pointed. "I think those are hills. Which means there's another side."

Eider shielded her eyes from the sun. Her heart fluttered. It had been too hazy to see before, but now that the wind had settled a bit, way off in the distance, she could make out the shape of land across the water.

It had been hazy when Teacher had brought her here, too, Eider remembered. Teacher had probably planned it that way.

"Then what is this?" she asked. "Where are we?"

"I don't know," Finch said. "But if we walk along the edge of this—of this sea—I bet we'll find something. Maybe even the other side."

———

They continued along the sea-that-wasn't. South, then southwest as the shoreline gradually began to curve around.

Eider kept glancing back to make sure they weren't being followed. She didn't see anybody. But that didn't mean they weren't coming.

They found an old cement dock, half crumbled into the water. A door with no house attached. An ancient pillar crusted with white. Each discovery made Eider feel more nervous. Like the end of the world—the nobody and the nothing—was larger and realer than she'd thought.

But then, what had the ketchup been? The stiff but edible bread?

"So what's our destination, anyway?" Finch asked.

"Destination?"

"Where are we headed after this?"

"Good question." Eider felt shy, all of a sudden. She reached into her overalls pocket and pulled out the housing-development pamphlet. "I was thinking maybe this place," she said, handing it over.

"*Huge front lawns*," Finch read. "What's a *gazebo*?"

"No clue."

"Where did you find this?"

"A few weeks ago, when I was out exploring." Eider turned over the pamphlet. "See, there's a little map. The *W* is for *west*. Teacher said there's a highway west of here— this long road might be it, right?" She traced the path with her finger. "After it crosses this other road, there'll be a bridge. . . ."

Finch didn't look convinced. "But we don't know if we're near the highway at all. Or how old this map is."

"It looks newer than my other papers."

"You had other papers?"

"Well, yeah. I had lots."

"Why didn't you ever show me?"

Eider shrugged. "You were keeping stuff from me, too. All the plans and ideas in your notebooks."

"But I—" Finch paused. "Yeah. I guess we all kept stuff from each other."

They shared a can of bright yellow pineapple chunks, then continued southwest along the sea. Their shadows grew longer and longer.

Part of Eider welcomed the night. The temperature would be cooler. And they could hide much more easily in the dark. But other things could hide more easily, too.

Dangerous things, just waiting for them to fall asleep. Eider wished she could switch off her thoughts, but she couldn't. She chewed and chewed her thumbnails.

And then she burst out, "I'm scared about Robin. About finding her." She paused. "I'm scared we won't."

"It's been years," Finch said carefully.

"I know. And it's dangerous out here. Teacher said . . ." Eider wiped her eyes. "Teacher said there's no way she could have survived."

"Well . . . nothing bad has happened to us."

"But we've only been out here a day. If the world still exists—all the bridges and buildings and pangolins and armadillos—doesn't that mean dangerous things still exist, too?"

"I guess."

"Maybe there are worse snakes than rattlesnakes. And worse creatures than snakes."

"Maybe," Finch said.

Eider peered at him. "Why don't you seem nervous?"

"I'm not really sure. I always was before. But now that we're out here . . ." He shrugged, a grin tugging at his cheeks. "Wow. You know?"

Because she couldn't help it, Eider smiled too. "I guess it is kind of amazing."

"And we haven't even gone that far!"

It was true. They were still in the desert. With the same desert sounds, the same desert sameness—which, in a strange way, was comforting. Even the stink was comforting, because Eider knew it came from the sea. Or *a* sea. A dying sea that was most likely—probably—not the ocean.

The ocean still existed. And so did they.

And so did Robin. Eider believed it, as strongly as she'd ever believed anything. She *felt* her. A warmth tightening Eider's chest, as if they were connected heart to heart, no matter where her sister was.

How far could a kid walk in three years?

29
REAL LEADERS

EIDER LAY WITH HER HEAD ON HER PACK, trying to sleep. Finch was keeping first watch. She could hear him tinkering with whatever junk he'd found.

Suddenly, her eyes sprang open. "Do you hear that?"

Finch inhaled sharply. "Oh no."

Eider sat up. Right away, she saw it: the van. Crunching over the ground, its big, knobby tires flattening sagebrush and whatever creatures lived inside. It had found them. Or maybe it had been following them this whole time. Like the predatory cats they'd read about in World Book C, waiting until they were tired.

"Should we run?" Eider scrambled to put her boots back on. Why had she taken them off? Why had she felt secure, even for a second?

"We'll never make it," Finch said fearfully. "We're the worst runners."

"No, Linnet's the worst runner."

"Now we definitely won't make it."

Eider ran a few steps in her unlaced boots, then gave up as the van crunched to a stop a few yards away. For some reason, it looked crooked. Then she noticed one of the tires was much smaller, like the ones on the Handyman's truck.

"Jay must have slashed it," Finch said. "No wonder it took them so long."

"Not long enough."

They both shut up as the van's doors opened. Eider wondered if she should pick up a rock to defend them. But she wasn't Jay, the strongest. Just like she wasn't Avis, the most agile, or Finch, the smartest. She was only Eider: more scared than she'd ever felt.

Nurse climbed out first, a sheen of sweat on his flat, bald head. "Oh, you silly, foolish kids," he began, then stopped as Teacher slammed the door.

"You made it pretty far this time," she said. "No snake-bites, I hope?"

She sounded concerned—or rather, like she was *trying* to sound concerned. Crocodile concern, Eider thought. Like Robin's crocodile tears. Because now, Eider knew Teacher's anger was there, steaming just below the surface.

Had it always been there? Was that why Teacher kept them away from the world? Not only them—but herself, too. Teacher had given up the world. For a second, Eider thought of the framed photo she'd seen in Teacher's office.

She had no idea what had happened to them—to Teacher's family. But there were lots of ways for the world to end. Eider knew that firsthand.

"Finch," Teacher said. "I'm so disappointed in you."

Finch shuffled his feet.

"And Eider. After all the chances I've given you. How could you?"

How couldn't *I?* Eider wanted to say. But she felt too defeated.

"I know which one of you was behind this. It's not the first time, after all. But it's definitely going to be the last. We'll have a talk back at the ranch." Teacher paused. "A big one this time."

Eider couldn't look at Teacher, so she glared at Nurse instead. He just stood there—obviously distraught, but not speaking up, either. Which was almost as bad.

Teacher slid open the door of the van.

Avis sat inside.

Her eyes were red-rimmed, her cheeks puffy. Like she'd been crying ever since she'd last seen Eider. Ever since she'd squeezed her hand good-bye. Ever since Eider had told her which direction they were headed.

Eider's mouth fell open. "You told them where we went."

"I'm sorry," Avis whispered. "I'm so sorry."

"How could you, Avis?"

"I didn't have a choice! You know I didn't."

"Yes, you did," Eider said furiously.

Maybe Teacher hadn't allowed them to make big decisions. But they made choices, every single day. Everyone did. You could choose to trust. You could choose to listen. You could choose to believe. There were options.

Eider climbed into the back of the van, sitting as far from Avis as possible. Finch climbed in beside her, and Teacher slammed the door behind them. After a moment, the engine started. The cold air barely reached them through the metal grate dividing them from the front seats.

She watched the desert sameness, or what she could see of it, pass through the dusty widows. As they headed back to the desert ranch, away from the possibilities of Beyond. Away from the reality of Robin.

"Maybe if I'd been a real leader," Eider said to Finch. "Maybe then we'd have made it."

"You *are* a real leader," Finch said.

"No, I'm not. I could have gotten us out of here if I was a real leader. I keep making the wrong decisions. And I've been scared the whole time."

"Who says real leaders aren't scared? I bet they're terrified. The good ones, I mean. If they aren't, then maybe they're just crazy."

Eider thought about that.

"It will be okay, Eider," Avis said. "We'll get through this. All of us will."

No, Eider wouldn't. And neither would Teacher—Eider was certain of that. Teacher would discipline her. Take everything she'd ever loved. Pinch and prod her brain like clay, until it became something else entirely. Find other ways to make her forget Robin had ever existed.

Or maybe Teacher would make the other kids forget *Eider* had ever existed. If she'd done it once, she could do it again.

Eider was scared. Eider was terrified.

She was scared of making the wrong decision. But she was terrified of not making the right one.

She unbuckled her seat belt and scrambled over Finch's lap. "What are you doing?" he asked.

She slid open the van door. The desert sameness sped by. Fast, but not too fast. A jump would hurt, but maybe not too much. Not as much as not jumping. The hardest part was the first step. Only in this case, it was a very big step.

"Don't!" Avis cried.

Eider leaped.

She soared.

IT ALL HAPPENED SO FAST. The jump. The slam of the earth, the pain of gravel in Eider's hands and knees. She somersaulted and somehow found her feet. They started running as soon as she was vertical.

"Eider!"

She whirled around. Finch—or maybe it was Avis—had thrown Eider her pack. She dove for it, looping her arms through the straps. She head Teacher yell, but Nurse didn't slow the van. Was he standing up to Teacher at last?

It didn't matter. Eider was off.

All her training, all her days of exploration in the desert ranch's outskirts had made her familiar with the desert terrain. She knew what kind of slope would send her skidding. Which earth was firm and which she'd punch through. She knew what brush she could step into and what she should step over, or avoid entirely. It was an Extrasensory all her own, a language she didn't even have to think about.

She spoke it in her bones.

—

Eider had never run this long before. A few loops around the fence during Physical, a handful of tries at the obstacle course. Enough to know a pinch in her side, a burn in her throat, an ache in her calves. But just barely.

Now she knew those sensations had just been beginnings. The twin pricks from a snakebite that kept biting, biting, biting, until white-hot pain was all she knew.

Okay, maybe it wasn't *that* bad.

But by the time she reached the first big outcrop of rock, it might have been the second-worst pain of her life. She skidded to a stop, then ducked into the shade. It wasn't very much shade. She had to stoop. For a moment, she wondered if it was the same outcrop she and Robin had found. No, they hadn't made it this far.

Frantic for water, she opened her pack and reached inside. The first thing she touched was unfamiliar. She pulled it out.

Finch's radio.

So that was what he'd been tinkering with earlier. And he must have tossed her his pack instead of hers. But the radio was broken, wasn't it?

She examined it. Surprisingly, it seemed all right. She tapped the wires and swiveled the dial like Finch had. It turned on—but all she heard was the low crackle-hum. She switched it off. She drank half a bottle of water. As soon as she stood, the silence hit her like a huge, crashing wave.

She was alone.

For the first time in her entire life. She was alone.

Eider had thought she'd been alone before. But she hadn't been, not truly. Even if none of the other kids could match the bond she'd shared with Robin, they'd been friends—better friends than she'd realized. They'd been family.

Now they were gone. And Eider had to be leader of herself.

"Which way?" she asked.

She stood with her hands on her hips, considering the sun. Like she had three years ago, with Robin at her side.

The sun came from the east each morning. But that was where the night came from, too. The dark, and all that it entailed. Heading west meant walking with the sun.

"West," she replied. "Away from the night."

And maybe toward Robin.

—

Eider hiked and hiked. She ate half a can of cold, squishy beans and hiked. The midday sun clawed at her shoulders. She tied her jacket over them like a cape and hiked.

When she couldn't bear another step, she took another. And then another. Until every single step became her last, then last, then last.

It helped to think she was following Robin's footsteps. Of course, Eider had no way of knowing if she was really tracking her sister's path. Any actual footprints would have blown away years ago. But the idea of them was there, haunting the desert sameness.

Except . . . the desert wasn't really the same anymore.

The change had come so gradually, Eider hadn't noticed. There were more rocks, now. More color to the weeds, and more plants overall. Some were so big they were practically trees.

She lifted her water to her lips and swallowed. From the rise before her, she heard a scuffle-clatter. She froze—then giggled.

It was only a kit fox.

Kit foxes had visited the desert ranch time to time, but the mean dog had always frightened them off. Or Nurse had, when they'd ransacked the garbage pail.

Eider grinned at the fox, which stared back. It had a tiny, pointed snout, and its ears were comically huge in comparison. Goofy kit fox ears. Its large, dark eyes almost reminded her of Robin's.

"Hello," Eider said.

With a lightning-quick flash of tail, the kit fox took off. Eider jogged a few steps after it, then realized she had no idea where the little animal had gone.

She felt even more alone.

"But not for long," she said out loud. "I won't be alone for much longer."

Because if she said it out loud, it was real.

"I'm thirsty," she said out loud.

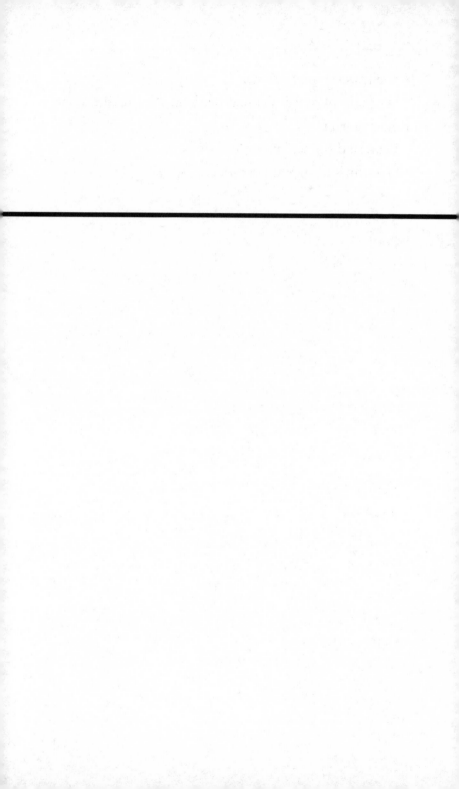

31

BIRDSONG

EIDER WOKE TO A WHOOSHING SOUND.

It was the strangest sensation. Not the sound, but the waking. Because she didn't remember going to sleep. If she had gone to sleep on purpose, she certainly wouldn't have lain down like this, with her chin in the dirt.

"Ugh," she said, sitting up. All her muscles ached. She brushed the dirt from her chin and stomach, then froze.

Whoosh. Whoosh. Whoosh.

In the hazy gray morning, something moved. Something *huge*. Not just one, but many—a dozen or more, spread out across the desert panorama before her. White spikes with white arms that slowly spun. Like robot angels. They were the biggest things Eider had ever seen.

She had no idea if they were dangerous. Should she be scared? She didn't *feel* scared. Maybe because they seemed familiar, somehow. . . .

Windmills!

Like the ones on the ranch. So they were generating electricity—tons of electricity, judging by their size.

Eider stood on a ridge and watched them, the robot angel windmills. They were nearly silent, like the seabirds she'd seen. Barely a whisper of sleek white wings. Capturing energy from the air. But energy for what? Something big, that was for sure.

Then she noticed a white flutter, riding the same breeze that spun the windmills. She hurried over and grabbed it. Only a napkin, but it made her smile. A moment later, she spotted something else—dark, this time, and larger.

"Ha!" she exclaimed, picking it up.

It was another housing-development pamphlet, exactly like her other one. Was it a coincidence? Or did it have deeper meaning?

Was she getting close?

Eider stuffed it into her pack and hiked onward.

——

The desert sameness changed into other kinds of sameness, until nothing around Eider was the same at all.

The ground sloped and rose until it became hills and valleys, pitching and rolling all around her. The ground grew rockier. The rocks grew larger. Before she knew it, she was weaving through boulders.

The hills were covered in boulders, too: big lumpy things, like the giants in her fairytale book. As if at any moment, they might unfold from where they crouched, unfurl their rocky arms, and bellow into the sky.

Shade was easy to find now, as Eider hiked around the boulders. But even in the sun, it wasn't as hot. And there were green things everywhere. Even actual trees.

Then she heard a soft, electric murmur, not unlike the sound of Finch's radio. She followed it to the tiniest, narrowest brook, trickling between a cleft in the rocks.

"Water!" she yelled.

Her bottle wouldn't fit, so she cupped her hands in the water and lifted it to her face. It was like drinking dreams. Moonlight and shooting stars.

Eider stayed there ten minutes, slowly slurping, until at last she'd had her fill. Then she sank down beside the brook, her back against a boulder. She felt content. Not only content—safe, in her maze of boulders.

What would happen if she climbed one?

Once she'd thought it, she knew she had to. She scaled a lower boulder, then another. She was careful—*so* careful. If she hurt herself, there would be nobody to help her this time. Slowly, she stood.

She was on top of the world.

A world so vast, so colorful and dizzying, Eider instantly dropped into a crouch. She waited until her knees stopped shaking, then stood again.

In front of her, the boulder-strewn hills lumped and folded and spread out, high and low, brown and green, rolling forever into the distance. A hazy distance, but even greener.

She saw vast canyons and high hills, maybe mountains.

She saw a road! A big one. It was far away, but it was definitely a road. With automobiles moving on it, she thought.

She saw dozens and hundreds and millions of things. She saw the whole wide world in front of her. Where it has always been.

But what about behind her?

Carefully, she turned.

The difference was startling. The boulder-strewn hills receded sooner than she'd thought, for how long she'd hiked. And after that, there was only desert. Layers of beige, rolling, then crumbling like crushed fish bones into the sea. Which she could see from here, too: the sea that wasn't the sea. She knew how huge it was, up close. But from way up here, it looked like a lake. A pond. A puddle.

How had she ever mistaken it for the real sea? The clear blue sea with huge, crashing waves?

Eider turned west again, facing the whole wide world. Somewhere, the real sea still existed. The ocean. She believed it was there, even if she couldn't see it. More than ever before, she wished she could spread her arms and soar for real. As beautiful as the world was, she still had to cross it. She had a long way to go.

But maybe not so long anymore.

"ROBIN!" Eider screamed at the top of her lungs.

Her voice bounced from boulder to boulder, spreading through the hills like the sweetest birdsong. For a split second, Robin was everywhere. Ringing in Eider's ears, even as she climbed back down.

———

Back in her shady place, Eider remembered Finch's radio.

She got it out and cradled it on her lap. Turned it on and swiveled the dial. Tapped the wires. Then she paused. Sounds she'd never heard before tickled her eardrums.

Music. It was music!

Eider swiveled the dial again. She heard a man's voice—he was talking about sushi. That made her laugh. Another swivel: more music, this time with a thumping beat and a woman's voice singing. She couldn't understand the words—maybe they were in a different language.

So many people broadcasting. Did that mean Eider was close to a real town? She hadn't seen one from up above, but those automobiles had to be heading somewhere.

She turned the dial a little more. And then she heard another voice—not singing, but talking. A voice she knew. But not Teacher's.

"—we're here. We're the kids at the desert ranch, out past the sea. We're all okay, but we need help. . . ."

It was her friends.

32

LIKE A FOX

EIDER'S CIRCADIAN RHYTHMS HAD GONE ALL WONKY.

She walked and slept, sometimes for a couple hours and sometimes longer, in the dark and in the light. She wasn't sure which she preferred. The daytime wasn't so hot anymore, but the night didn't seem as frightening.

Especially as she walked beside the big road. There weren't many automobiles at night. In the daytime, they moved scary-quick. Zooming toward her in an ever-increasing rush, until they passed with a *ROAR!* and the rush faded.

But it wasn't just the speed that made her nervous. It was the Other People inside. If they saw her and stopped— how could Eider know they weren't dangerous?

There was no way of knowing. She'd trusted Teacher, after all.

But she kept the road in sight, or at least in mind. Always to her right as she walked, hiked, climbed.

Once, Eider realized she was walking into a canyon—the ground had descended so gradually, she hadn't noticed. She trudged back toward the road. When she reached the top, she realized it was nearing a second road. Not far ahead, they crossed.

She pulled out her pamphlet and looked at the map.

When she glanced up again, her heart jerked. An automobile had pulled over, just as she'd feared. Before she could figure out what to do, the window rolled down. A woman with curly blond hair leaned out.

"Hey!" the woman said. "Are you okay?"

Eider wondered if she should run. But the woman didn't look dangerous. Unlike Teacher's crocodile concern, hers seemed genuine.

"I'm—" Eider's voice came out a dusty croak. She cleared her throat and tried again. "I'm fine."

"Are you sure? You're pretty far outside of town."

Town? She was near a town? "How far?"

"Almost a mile."

Eider didn't have to fake her grin. A mile was nothing. "Oh, okay! I'll head back right now."

"Want me to drive you there?"

Talking to Other People was one thing. Climbing in somebody's automobile was another. "No, that's all right. I like walking." Eider paused. "But by any chance . . . do you have some water?"

"You're in luck." The woman rummaged around, then held a water bottle out the window. "Next time, bring your own, okay?"

Eider nodded. Then she turned and ran back into the canyon, skidding and sliding, but managing to stay on her desert-trained feet. She waited until the automobile drove away before climbing back out. Still grinning.

A town! She was on the right track.

———

Then came the bridge, arching over the canyon. It was unlike anything Eider had ever imagined, but dreamlike just the same. She walked along its edge, trying not to look down. Halfway across, she glanced at her map again. The housing development should be right on the other side.

She didn't see the housing development.

But she saw buildings. Lots of them. And roads, criss-crossing in all different directions. She didn't know where to go, or where to look. Her head spun, and part of her felt like throwing up.

"What's up?"

It was a pair of boys, sitting on a bench. They both held sandwiches, which made Eider's mouth water. She'd finished the last of her food a day ago. "Nothing," she muttered, then hurried away.

After a second, she slowed. Before her nervousness could take over, she turned around and came back.

"Could you please tell me where all the houses are?" she asked the boys.

"Houses?" one of them repeated.

She held out her pamphlet. "These ones."

"Ah, the new construction." The other boy pointed his sandwich. "Just down that road. When you get to the end, hang a right."

Eider was exhausted. Battered by every type of emotion. But somehow, her legs were running again. Down the road. Colors and textures flashed by on either side, walls and windows and rooftops. But she kept running. At the end of the road, she turned right—where she saw a sign.

Welcome Home!

The same happy, swirly letters as in Eider's pamphlet. She had arrived!

But . . . there were no homes. Only skeletons.

For a moment, Eider wondered if the world really had ended. But she knew for a fact that wasn't true.

The houses weren't broken-down like the ruins she'd seen in the desert. But they weren't homes, either. They were spines and ribs. She could see right through from room to room. Concrete for floors, like the slabs. Sometimes, no ceilings at all.

She walked down the street, between the skeleton houses, her heart sinking and sinking. The homes weren't the only thing the pamphlet had gotten wrong. The images had showed big, bushy trees. But here, there were no trees. No flowers. No green, grassy lawns.

No sky-blue couches with families on them.

No happily ever after.

Eider knew she'd been silly to hope. But she'd come so far. She'd been through so much. And now she'd reached the end of her plan.

With nothing else to do, she kept walking. At the end of the street, she reached a fence. The gate wasn't pad-locked, so she pushed it open—and saw a massive hole in the ground. It was edged in ceramic squares. Eider stepped closer, peering inside.

Suddenly, someone grabbed her and yanked her back-ward. Before Eider could scream, the person let her go.

"You almost fell in! Not the best idea, with the water still missing."

It was a girl, close to Eider's age. Her skin was dark, like Linnet's, and her hair was wound in two neat bunches on her head. She wore a bright red coat with crisscrossing lines running through it. And she was smiling.

"What is it for?" Eider asked. "The hole?"

"Supposed to be our community swimming pool," the girl said. "My family's going to move into one of these houses. If they ever finish them, that is. Are you going to live here too?"

"No, I just . . . I saw the papers. The glossy ones."

"Oh, those!" The girl shoved up her sleeves to the elbow, but they immediately fell forward again. "I'm pretty sure they're what convinced my parents. Do you live near here?"

At that, Eider had to laugh. "I live very far away," she said, then paused. "Lived."

"How far away? No offense, but . . . you're kind of a mess."

Eider glanced down at herself. She *was* a mess. Dirt caked her boots. Her overalls and arms, too. She had no idea what her hair looked like, but it was probably a fright.

"Are you all right?" the girl asked.

Eider nodded. But the girl kept staring at her, with the strangest expression.

"The thing is," she said, "you look like somebody I know. Or somebody I used to know—I haven't seen her in a while."

" 'Her'?"

"Yeah, a little girl."

Time stood still. Eider swallowed. "A little girl?"

"Not super little, but younger than us. Her eyes and hair and skin are just like yours. And something about your faces . . ." The girl pushed back her plaid sleeves again. "Do you have any cousins?"

"No," Eider said. "No cousins."

"Her brother's my best friend." She paused. "Well, he was my best friend."

A brother? Eider's hope died in her chest like a fallen bird. She felt like crying, but didn't want to embarrass herself.

"She was adopted, though. They look nothing alike. Not like the two of you do."

"Adopted?" Eider repeated. How did she know that word? Then she remembered—from one of the torn-out World Book pages she'd found. Something Teacher hadn't wanted her to know about. The scar on her ankle twinged.

"Yeah. I wish I could take you to meet her, but she's not here anymore."

"Do you know where she is?"

The girl shook her head. "But my friend might know. Do you want to meet him? I mean, it'll be kind of awkward—we didn't part ways on the best note."

Eider shrugged, then nodded. "Okay."

"Why don't you hop up on my handlebars?"

When Eider paused, the girl tapped between the handles of her bike. "Oh," Eider said, and climbed on.

"I'm Alice, by the way."

"I'm Eider."

"Eider! I've never heard that name before."

"Me neither," Eider said, holding on tight. "What's her name? The little girl?"

"Kit," Alice replied.

"Oh," Eider said again, trying to keep the disappointment from her voice. Then, because it was becoming an emergency, "Alice? Is there anywhere I could go to the bathroom?"

"Sure," Alice said, giggling. "There's a gas station a couple blocks away. The bathroom door's always unlocked."

A few minutes later, they pulled up beside a low, squat building. Signs in the windows read SUPERLOTTO TICKETS SOLD HERE! and ICE-COLD BEER! Eider didn't understand either one, but she figured that was a feeling she'd have to get used to.

Alice pointed to a door that said WOMEN. "No offense," she said, "but while you're in there, you might want to wash your face. You look like you fell in the Salton Sea or something."

The Salton Sea?

Eider shut the door behind her. She stared at herself in the cracked, foggy mirror. She was dirty—dirtier than she'd ever been.

Luckily, the water from the faucet poured and poured. She stuck her head under it and drank. Then she used a whole stack of papers to scrub her face, her neck, her arms all the way up to the elbows. The rest of her would have to wait.

Eider looked at herself in the mirror again. At her eyes and hair and skin.

"Kit," she said out loud. "Like a fox."

—

"Want me to take you the scenic route?" Alice asked as Eider climbed back onto her handlebars. "You'll get to see more of town that way."

"Okay," Eider agreed. Her scar twinged and twinged. As if she'd somehow pressed a button under her skin. Switched it on.

It really was a town. A *real* town. Not a fairytale village or an end-of-the-world city, but a real, normal town. With banks and a post office. More gas stations. Grocery stores and restaurants. *Fast-food* restaurants!

"My school's right over there," Alice said. "Where do you go to school?"

"Where I live," Eider said. "Lived."

"So you're homeschooled? That's such a coincidence! My friend used to be homeschooled, too. His sister—the one you look like—still was. Maybe because she doesn't talk."

"She doesn't talk?"

Alice didn't answer right away. "Oh, sorry," she said. "I forgot you can't see me shake my head. No, she doesn't talk. Or she didn't to me, anyway. I never knew why. . . ."

Don't say anything, Eider had said.

Not a word, until I find you.

The hand around her heart tightened. She held her eyes closed, then looked again. And looked. And looked.

There was so much to take in. So much! Eider tried to concentrate, to focus her senses the way she'd been taught in Extrasensory, but it was impossible. Finally, she relaxed. She let everything crash into her in an infinite wave, sparkling and colorful and noisy and terrifying and so, so exciting. The world. The real world. Real life.

It was here.

It had always been here. When Eider was hopping through obstacle courses and learning to see in the dark, it was here. When she was in bed with rattlesnake fever and crying over Robin, it was here. All these people were here, going about their daily lives in the real world that still existed. Had always existed.

Would continue to exist for a long, long time. Maybe forever.

The endless world.

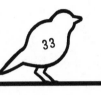

WISH YOU WERE HERE

ONCE THEY REACHED THE EDGE OF TOWN AGAIN, they rode through a grove of trees. Trees like Eider had never imagined. They were vastly tall and shaggy, with a tangy-strong scent like Nurse's cough medicine.

They reached another bridge, a lot like the one Eider had hurried across.

"Almost there," Alice called.

They passed through more of the fragrant trees. Then they were riding over a narrow, dirt-packed road. Up ahead, Eider saw a mailbox that read BIRCH.

"I'm about to stop again," Alice said.

Eider hopped off the bike. Before them stood a house: a big house, made of weathered gray wood, with empty fields all around it. She reached down and scratched her scar, but the twinging wouldn't quit.

Alice set the bike on its side. "Hope his stepdad's not home. I've never met him, but apparently he's a real weirdo. Into lots of end-of-the-world stuff. Crazy radio broadcasts and whatnot."

"Radio broadcasts?" Eider's head was spinning. "What's that over there? Where the land drops away?"

"That's part of the canyon," Alice said. "Can you imagine living with it in your backyard? Imagine how scary it'd be at night. I'd always wonder if something was living inside it. . . ."

Eider frowned at the canyon. There definitely could be things hiding down there. People, even. It wasn't so hard to hide from the world, even right here in town. You didn't need a desert to do it.

"Sorry," Alice said. "I've got a reputation for letting my imagination run away with me. Let's go."

They approached the big, old house. Eider's heart thumped louder with every step. Each one—not just the first—was the hardest.

Alice knocked on the door. They waited. The house was quiet. "Maybe none of them are home," she said, knocking a second time.

Eider bit her thumbnail.

And then the door opened.

A boy stood in the doorway. A boy even paler than Finch, with blue shadows under his eyes, which looked like they'd seen a lot. His hair was a shade between blond and brown. His clothes were disheveled, and he wore boots like Eider's—just as dirty, actually. It made her feel less self-conscious about the state of her own clothes, although she was glad she'd had the chance to wash her face.

"Hi, Alice," he said.

Then he saw Eider.

"Who . . ." The boy began. His eyes widened, which made him look like an owl. That was fine with Eider. She liked owls. "Are you from the desert ranch?"

"The desert ranch?" Alice repeated.

"My mom and I heard about it on the radio," the boy said. "Are you Eider?"

Eider hesitated, then nodded.

"They talked about you! The kids on the radio. My name's Jory. I . . ." He trailed off. "I'm sorry. You just look like . . ."

"Her," Eider said. "I look like her. I know."

"And—and you're wearing overalls. She was wearing them, too, when she—"

"When she left."

"When she got here."

It was too good be true, but it felt exactly right. The same way Eider had felt the entire scroll of world history unfurling. Except this time it was Eider's history.

Eider's fairytale.

EVER AFTER

ONCE UPON A TIME, EIDER'S WORLD HAD ENDED.

Once upon a time, it began again.

Or it was about to, anyway. Eider sat with her hands clasped over her knees. They'd cleaned her scrapes and cuts, and covered them with bandages. One had a yellow bird on them. He was tall, with big orange legs. He seemed kind of freaky, Eider thought.

Beside her, Jory jiggled his foot. He kept glancing at her, then away. Eider didn't mind. She looked like Robin, after all.

Protective Services thought the same thing. They were a pair of grown-ups with kind, concerned faces: a woman with curly hair and a man with smiling eyes, who'd given her candy that stuck in her teeth. "Sisters," they'd said. "No doubt about it."

They could see it as well as Alice could. The way Eider always had. Same olive-brown skin. Same dark hair. Same big eyes and cheeks, though Robin's had always been pinker. Eider missed her sister's cheeks.

Jory did, too. Eider could tell.

So did Jory's mother. The moment she'd seen Eider, her eyes had filled with tears. She'd brought Eider here, along with Jory and his little brother. Eider barely knew them, but she felt much braver with them sitting beside her.

Eider had done her best to explain about the desert ranch, which took hours. She described what it looked like. How her life there had been. Everything and everybody. Teacher, who'd made Protective Services shake their heads and squint. Nurse and the Handyman, with his mean dog. The other kids—her best friends.

They seemed so far away now. Finch and Linnet and Jay and Avis. Eider was so scared for them.

"We have units heading to the ranch right this minute," the woman from Protective Services had assured her. "Police officers, too. And an ambulance, even if they don't need it. They're going to be just fine, Eider. We promise."

Eider wanted to believe them. But she didn't know yet whether they kept promises.

They still had a big one to keep.

She glanced at the door again. She wished they'd left it open, so she could see down the hall. She couldn't see if anybody was approaching. All her Extrasensory lessons, all her gifts and abilities, all her so-called specialness and not-specialness were useless against that door. Still, she concentrated, willing it to open.

And then it did.

Everybody in the room stood. Protective Services, and Jory's mom, and Jory, too. And Eider. She stood without even knowing it, as her sister entered the room.

Not skipping or dancing, but cautious, uncertain. Hair like a blackbird's wing. Eyes like a kit fox's. Cheeks like a robin's breast. All of her so very much like Eider, and yet so much her own self, too.

She saw Jory first. Her face lit up.

Then she saw Eider.

Instantly, her smile froze. Her large, dark eyes filled with tears. Eider could see the sparkle from across the room.

She looked from Eider to Jory. And back again. Her hesitation hung in the air, along with the big question: who she'd go to first.

Her sister Eider.

Or her brother Jory.

It only lasted a moment, though. Because they both ran to her instead.

DON'T MISS JORY'S STORY

WATCH THE SKY

KIRSTEN HUBBARD